Ghost Lagoon

Redemption Mountain, Book Twenty-Five

Historical Western Romance

SHIRLEEN DAVIES

Books Series by Shirleen Davies

Historical Western Romances
Redemption Mountain
MacLarens of Fire Mountain Historical
MacLarens of Boundary Mountain

Contemporary Western Romance
Cowboys of Whistle Rock Ranch
MacLarens of Fire Mountain Contemporary
Macklins of Whiskey Bend

Romantic Suspense
Eternal Brethren Military Romantic Suspense
Peregrine Bay Romantic Suspense

Find all my books at: shirleendavies.com

The best way to stay in touch is to subscribe to my newsletter. Go to my Website *www.shirleendavies.com* and fill in your email and name in the Join My Newsletter boxes. That's it!

Description

She's a divorced mother and teacher in a growing frontier town.
He's a deputy with no intention of forming a relationship beyond friendship.
Will the return of her ex and the appearance of a handsome stranger change his mind?

Dutch McFarlin accepts his job as a deputy in the bustling frontier town of Splendor, Montana, and solitary nights will guide each day. Although the town has several eligible, single women who've shown an interest in him, he's content as a bachelor, seeing no reason to change. Not until a divorced mother begins to control his thoughts and heart.

Dorinda Heaton thrives in her teaching position and being a mother to her young son. Her days are filled with challenges, few greater than the reappearance of her former husband. She's forgiven him for breaking a solemn promise, though her trust in the man she still loves is shattered. Uncertain she'll ever remarry, she forges a strong bond with Dutch, relying on the man to be her guiding light, and possibly more.

Faced with a growing number of challenges, their friendship grows. When unknown threats hit close to home, they rely on each other for support and advice, neither realizing how tight their bond is becoming.

Just as their lives begin to calm, their friendship faces another test. A stranger rides into Splendor, displaying a pointed interest in Dorinda. The man's attention forces Dutch to reevaluate his view of the future, and imagine what it would be like without her in his life.

Will the revelation convince Dutch to change his path and confess his feelings? Or has he waited too long to acknowledge what he should've known all along?

Ghost Lagoon, book twenty-five in the Redemption Mountain historical western romance series, is a full-length, clean and wholesome novel with an HEA and no cliffhanger.

Table of Contents

Ghost Lagoon

Prologue

Bison City
Idaho Territory, 1866

"What do you see?" Luke Pelletier held his position as Dutch McFarlin peeked over the edge of the window, watching and listening to the conversation taking place inside.

Dutch had been with the Pinkerton Detective Agency for well over a year, while Luke had been recruited a month before. It was supposed to be one quick job—in and out.

Weeks later, Luke found himself embroiled in a string of events that threatened to go on for months if he and his partner didn't end it tonight.

"Flatnose and at least ten of his men," Dutch hissed, keeping his voice low. They'd followed Dave Flatnose Darvis to the remote hideout after a tip from a member of the local vigilante committee or, as they preferred to call themselves, the Citizens Committee.

Flatnose and his men were suspected of robbing a series of gold transport wagons, stealing the treasure, and killing anyone who resisted. The death count stood at two confirmed. The trouble was no one had any firm proof Flatnose's gang was behind any of the crimes, and no one could identify the leader. The outlaws had been careful to hide their faces behind bandanas and hats pulled low across their foreheads. The only clue to his identity had been a slip by one of his men during a holdup. A guard swore he'd heard the man call their leader Flatnose.

The good people of Bison City established the Citizens Committee after the killing of the two guards. It hadn't taken them long to hire the Pinkerton Agency. Dutch arrived a couple weeks before Luke, contacting his friend when it appeared a second agent would be needed and Pinkerton had no one available to send.

In truth, Luke had jumped at the chance to get away from the ranch and give his brother, Dax, and new wife, Rachel, some privacy. Besides, Luke needed time to figure out his own future.

If they could find the proof, Luke would be on the road back to his ranch in Montana tomorrow, ending his relationship with Allan Pinkerton and his illustrious agency, at least for the moment.

"Darn," Dutch murmured, and dropped down, scooting behind some bushes as two men stepped onto the porch. He recognized Flatnose Darvis from a game of cards at a Bison City saloon. He heard Flatnose had earned his nickname during a fight when his opponent slammed a shovel into his face. Dutch didn't recognize the second man, who reached into a pocket, pulled out a slim cheroot, and lit it, blowing the smoke out in a long stream.

"The committee has hired someone from Pinkerton's to find out who's behind the robberies," the man standing next to Flatnose said. No one knew him by his real name, Frederick Marlowe, or his connection to Flatnose. Few knew he and Darvis were equal partners. And no one, except Flatnose, knew his last name. The men called him Rick.

"Where'd you hear that?" Flatnose asked, lighting his own cigar.

"The mayor's daughter," Rick answered, recalling how easy it had been to flatter the information out of the naïve young woman. "She said they believe a gang, led by a man named Flatnose, was behind the thefts."

Flatnose let out a string of curses before taking a deep draw from his cigar.

"We should head back to Montana. There's more gold to be had closer to home, without the interference of the Pinkerton men." Rick didn't mention Star Ranch, even though both knew that's where he wanted to go.

The property consisted of several hundred acres he and Flatnose purchased after Rick's brief term as a lawman in the Dakota Territory. He'd learned a lot while in the job and applied much of it to the robberies they pulled afterward.

Flatnose looked out over the thick pine forest, finished his cigar, and ground it out under his boot. "Tell the boys we'll leave at first light."

Dutch moved toward the back of the cabin, where Luke covered a second entrance. He'd heard enough to believe Flatnose and his men were who they sought, but not enough to convict them. They'd need to find the gold or have one of the men confess.

"What now?" Luke asked as Dutch crouched next to him.

Dutch pulled out his pocket watch. "We've got six hours until daylight. That's when they plan to leave for Montana."

"Not much time to get what we need." Luke pushed his hat back on his head. "If they're leaving, the gold's got to be here. We need to catch them with it before they ride out."

"You know, the odds are in their favor. Twelve to two." Dutch felt the need to point out the obvious since he'd been the one to get Luke involved.

Luke and Dutch had served together in the Confederate Army, both ending up in the Confederate Secret Service Bureau, a covert group made up of military and civilian men and women.

"We've got four, maybe five hours before they make their move. We have two choices—ride back to Bison City to gather more men, or stay here and handle it our way."

"Have we ever faced odds like this before?" Luke asked.

"Never."

Luke pulled off his hat, speared his fingers through his dark auburn hair, and flashed a grin at Dutch. "Guess it's time we did. What's life without a little adventure?"

"Not worth living, in my opinion." Dutch smiled back. He checked his revolver, confirming it was loaded, then checked his second gun before picking up the Spencer repeating rifle he'd hidden a few feet away. "What's the plan?"

Luke positioned himself several yards away from where the gang had used a rope to string their horses. All remained saddled. The only item missing for a quick escape was the gold.

He could see Dutch crouched at the corner of the rickety house, checking his guns again and stifling a yawn. It had surprised both men to see no guards posted. Luke figured Flatnose had become more arrogant as time passed, and their crimes had gone undetected. He'd always believed stupidity played a key role in catching most outlaws.

He glanced up to see Dutch's signal, indicating movement inside. Not a minute later, several men walked out carrying saddlebags, plus small metal boxes balanced on their shoulders. They were silent as they trekked the short distance to their horses and secured their loads. Once finished, they started back inside, not once looking around, even though the early morning light made it easy to see.

As soon as they were out of sight, Luke moved with quiet confidence toward the horses. He checked the saddlebags on one horse, found nothing, then moved to the box. Surprised it had no lock, he lifted the lid to find it filled with gold. He quickly checked one more before signaling Dutch and reclaiming his position behind a stand of bushes a few yards away.

"Hurry up. We need to move," Flatnose's voice boomed through the quiet morning air. He stepped aside as several men walked past him, heading for their horses, and carrying more boxes.

Nine men stood with the horses, including Flatnose. Dutch signaled Luke as the last three men stepped out of the house and onto the porch.

"Hands up, gentlemen." Dutch leveled his six-shooter at the outlaws as their hands moved for their guns. "I wouldn't try it," he warned, and glanced toward Luke, who'd drawn his weapons and pointed them toward the men standing near Flatnose.

"Everyone stay where you are and don't move." Luke made his way toward the cover of a large boulder, where he'd left his rifle, keeping his eyes focused on Flatnose.

No one moved until a laugh broke out from one of the men Dutch had covered—the same man Dutch had seen with Flatnose hours before. "You really think you can take all of us?"

"Doesn't matter. You and Flatnose will be the first to die." Luke's words slipped out as shots blasted near the house. He shifted his gaze from Flatnose long enough to see two outlaws lying motionless. It was seconds too long.

Fifteen seconds seemed like minutes as bullets flew, men shouted, and bodies fell. Later, Luke wouldn't be able to recall how he'd made it behind the boulder with a wound to his head, or how Dutch had taken two hits and still remained alive. When he woke, he found himself face down in the dirt, a small pool of blood under his head.

Luke pushed to his feet, feeling nauseous and dizzy. He didn't stop moving until he found Dutch trying to tie a kerchief around the wound to his leg with his one good arm, the other one hanging useless.

"How many did we get?" Dutch's jaw clenched at the pain ripping through his body.

"I counted six, including the two on the porch."

"Five got away." Dutch rested his back against the house, angry they'd let so many escape.

"Why didn't they stay around to finish us?"

"You don't remember?"

Luke shot a disgusted look at Dutch before lowering himself to one of the porch steps and resting his head in his hands. "I don't remember much after you shot the first ones."

"Not a second passed before you plugged the two closest to you, then spun and hit one more. I hit another before taking shots in my leg and arm as Flatnose and the rest of his men mounted and took off. One of their bullets must have grazed your head."

Luke looked toward the bodies several yards away. "Guess I'd better load them on horses and deliver them to the sheriff, along with any gold the outlaws left behind."

"Then what?"

Luke leveled his gaze at Dutch. "If Pinkerton gives the okay, we follow them to Montana."

Chapter One

Splendor, Montana
Spring 1875

Dorinda strode the quiet streets of Splendor, Montana, her son, Joel, skipping along beside her. The cool spring breeze would soon turn warm, then cool again as the day progressed. This had become her favorite time of day when the streets were quiet. She paused to take in the sharp grandeur of the snow-capped mountains rising in the distance, thankful for the chance to start fresh in this frontier town.

"Morning, Miss Dorinda, Joel," came a familiar deep voice behind them.

Dorinda turned to see Deputy Dutch McFarlin falling into step, his tall frame casting a shadow over them. Though some townsfolk whispered about Dutch's mysterious past, Dorinda welcomed the comfort his stalwart presence created.

"Deputy McFarlin," Dorinda replied. "You're up and about early."

"With the town growing by the day, I seem to

wake up earlier and earlier," Dutch said, his brow furrowing. "Last night, some miscreants vandalized the general store. Stan Petermann is spitting mad the deputies patrolling at night didn't stop the destruction. We're stretched thin as it is. Unless the newly created town council doesn't approve the increased budget Gabe submitted, I'm not sure how we'll keep up if this lawlessness continues to spread."

Dorinda's smile faded. More rabble-rousers spelled trouble for the schoolhouse, too. She looked around for Joel, suddenly uneasy. Spotting him up ahead didn't ease her worry at Dutch's words.

Dutch saw the unease on her face when she glanced at him. "Not to worry, Miss Dorinda. Gabe will get the money approved for more deputies. Until then, they'll be more deputies patrolling at night."

Dorinda gave a sharp nod. Maybe Splendor wasn't as peaceful as she'd hoped, but she wouldn't be scared off that easily.

"We're grateful for your vigilance, Deputy." She glanced up to see the school in front of her, the other teacher, Amelia Wheeler, already standing by the open door. "If you'll excuse me, we need to review lesson plans. Will we see you at Suzanne's for supper?"

Dutch tipped his hat. "Wouldn't miss it. You two take care now."

Dorinda watched him continue his patrol. She learned something every time Dutch joined them for the walk to school. Today's lesson wasn't what she expected. Nevertheless, it was information she, and most of the town, would be wise to take to heart.

"Good morning," Amelia called cheerfully as Dorinda and Joel approached. "Are you ready to review the lesson plans?"

"I am." Dorinda stopped on the stoop. "Joel, why don't you play outside for a bit while Miss Amelia and I talk?"

"Yes, ma'am." Joel dashed down the steps as the two women entered the schoolhouse. They settled at one of the weathered desks, and Amelia spread out her papers.

"With more children arriving daily, we need to get creative," she said, shuffling through her notes. "I was thinking of dividing the older students into small groups for reading lessons. That would allow us time to work one-on-one with the younger children."

Dorinda nodded, impressed by Amelia's initiative. As they delved deeper, the sound of Joel's laughter drifted through the window, mingling with the morning bustle of the street.

"Well, now, you two look as busy as bees this fine morning."

Dorinda turned to see Charley Kelly, owner of the Splendor Herald, filling the doorway. He and his wife, Maude, had started publishing the newspaper two years after the previous owners left town.

"Good morning, Mr. Kelly." Dorinda walked toward him. "Just going over some lesson plans."

Charley took several steps inside. "Good to hear. With all the new families flocking to town, you ladies have your work cut out for you."

He peered out the window at Joel, who was en-grossed in a game of marbles with two other boys. "Your boy sure is growing, Miss Dorinda."

"He's full of energy, as always." Dorinda chuckled.

Charley nodded, his eyes crinkling at the corners. "Maude and I want to write a story about the school, and the teachers. Most people in town know you're under a lot of pressure to take on more children with little in the way of funds. We want to get the word out about your valiant efforts under difficult conditions."

"We'd love that, wouldn't we, Amelia?" Dorinda asked.

"It would help spread the word about the dwin-dling school resources," she answered.

"Except for one issue, Charley," Dorinda said.

"What is that?"

"It is critical you do not portray us as complain-ing. We can't do anything which would alienate the town leaders."

"You mean the new town council?" Charley smiled.

"The town council and people who have a signifi-cant say in what happens in Splendor. Our job is to teach, not whine about what we don't have. Will my condition be acceptable to you?"

"Yes, of course. I understand your concern. May we schedule a time for me to interview the two of you?"

Dorinda looked at Amelia, who shrugged. "Would tomorrow right after school fit into your schedule?"

"It's fine with me. I'll be here right after the children leave. Thank you." He touched the brim of his hat.

"Well, that was interesting," Amelia said.

"It certainly was. Shall we finish reviewing today's lessons?" Dorinda asked.

As Amelia suggested other ways to present lessons, a thought popped into Dorinda's head on engaging students of different ages and backgrounds. She shared an idea for an interactive geography lesson, using a hand-drawn map.

Amelia clapped her hands. "Oh, I love the idea."

A sudden surge of children's voices echoed from outside. Dorinda peeked out the window to see students rushing to form a line at the schoolhouse entrance.

"Ready for another day?" Amelia asked.

A grin lifted the corners of Dorinda's mouth. "Definitely."

Dorinda and Joel stepped through the doors of the boardinghouse restaurant, amazed at the number of people already occupying the tables. Joel clung to her side, shy in the crowd, while Deputy McFarlin followed behind.

"Good to see you all," called Suzanne Barnett, winding through the busy tables. Her smile lit up her face. "Go ahead and take the table by the window. I'll be over in two shakes."

They settled into the chairs with Dutch facing the entrance. The table's location gave them a view of the entire dining room. Removing his hat, he unfurled his long frame across from them.

"How are you two this evening?" he rumbled.

"I'm good," Joel answered while looking out the window at a group of children peering through the window of the general store.

Dorinda smoothed Joel's hair, smiling at a couple she knew.

Suzanne walked over. "Now, what can I get you folks tonight?"

Dutch deferred to Dorinda. "Ladies first."

"I'll have the chicken pot pie. With extra gravy, please."

"An excellent choice. And for you, Master Joel?"

"Fried chicken?"

"Fried chicken with potatoes and gravy?"

He nodded at her.

"And for you, Deputy?"

"I'll have the fried steak, potatoes, and gravy. And save all of us slices of your fig pie."

"No!" Joel blurted before clamping a hand over his mouth.

"That's right," Dutch said. "You don't like figs. Guess we'll have to eat your wonderful apple pie, Suzanne."

Dorinda grinned. Dutch always found a way to help Joel feel comfortable.

Their food arrived within minutes. As they chatted over their meals, Dorinda felt the day's stresses melt away. It had taken time for her to feel comfortable around the people in Splendor. She'd been accustomed to being surrounded by people of the Mormon faith, experiencing little contact with those outside her beliefs. The pain of leaving her husband, his second wife, and their farm outside Salt Lake City had plagued her for a long time. Her older brother, Spencer, Dutch, Amelia, and other friends had helped to ease the pain and embrace the new life she'd chosen.

When their slices of pie arrived, Joel dug in. She smiled at Dutch, who watched the boy swallow every bite, leaving a few tiny crumbs on his plate.

As always, Dutch insisted on paying the bill. She'd learned to simply thank him instead of protesting, knowing it pleasured him to treat her and Joel to an evening out.

"One of these days, I'll get the check before you do, Dutch McFarlin. Just you wait."

He chuckled. "I'd like to see you try, Miss Dorinda. I'm quicker on the draw than you think."

Their friendly bickering continued as they left the restaurant. Though Dutch was not courting her, his small generosities touched Dorinda. She knew they came from a place of genuine care for her and Joel.

The night air was cool and still, with stars glittering overhead as Dorinda took Joel's hand. His small fingers curled trustingly around hers. Dutch fell into step beside them, their footsteps sounding on the wood slats of the boardwalk.

As they neared Dorinda's house, the tranquility

was shattered by the sudden crack of gunshots. They rang out sharply from Frontier Street, shattering the silence.

Dorinda gasped, her heart lurching. Joel cried out in fear beside her. Without thinking, Dutch grabbed Dorinda's hand, pulling her and the boy close.

"Let's get to your house." His eyes scanned the dark street, one hand hovering near his holstered six-shooter. More shots cracked through the night. Shouts and commotion rose up ahead of them.

Dorinda's pulse pounded as they hurried toward her house. She clutched Joel tightly, murmuring reassurances neither of them truly felt. The racket grew louder. Glass shattered, horses whinnied, and men shouted into the night.

What was happening? Dorinda's thoughts raced, fear and questions tumbling through her mind. Dutch's solid presence steadied her as he guided them through the darkness. His jaw was set, eyes alert for any sign of danger.

He hurried them along, his grip firm yet gentle on Dorinda's arm. As they reached her front door, he paused, glancing back toward the chaotic sounds of Frontier Street.

"Get inside. I need to find out what's going on and help the deputies."

"Be careful, Dutch."

Dutch gave her arm a reassuring squeeze. "Stay inside, and you'll be fine," he promised.

She ushered Joel inside, bolting the door behind them. Wide-eyed and trembling, he clung to her skirt.

Pulling him close, she smoothed his hair as she led him toward the bedroom.

"Let's get you to bed. Dutch and the other deputies will sort everything out."

Joel continued to glance around as she tucked him under the covers. Pressing a kiss to his forehead, she returned to the living room. Peering out the front window into the dark streets, she shivered. Men's loud voices could still be heard, along with the occasional gunshot.

Dorinda clasped her hands together, praying for Dutch's safety. She longed to know what was happening but could only wait. The sounds of chaos persisted late into the night as darkness clung to the town of Splendor.

Chapter Two

Dorinda woke with a start, momentarily confused by the pale dawn light filtering through the living room curtains. She glanced around, realizing she'd fallen asleep on the sofa.

Then the memories of the previous night came rushing back. The gunshots and men shouting. Dutch racing off to help however he could. And now, the agonizing wait to learn what had happened.

She hurried to check on Joel. He was still asleep, his chest rising and falling in a steady rhythm. Dorinda brushed the hair from his forehead before retreating from the bedroom to make coffee and fix breakfast.

In the living room, she paused to look out the window. The streets showed no signs of the commotion from the night before. What had happened after Dutch left, and was the threat still lurking?

Dorinda bit her lip. She needed to know if Dutch was all right. Grabbing her shawl, she headed for the door, then hesitated with her hand on the knob. She couldn't leave Joel alone.

Hand still gripping the knob, a knock sounded, causing her to startle and take a quick step away. Pulling the door open, relief washed over Dorinda at the sight of the tall deputy, with dark red hair, standing on her doorstep.

"Dutch!"

Before she could stop herself, Dorinda threw her arms around him. Dutch staggered back in surprise before carefully extricating himself from her embrace.

Feeling her face heat, she stepped away, motioning for him to enter the house. "Thank the Lord you're all right."

"It'll take more than a few rowdy cowhands to bring me down," he said. His tone was light, but she saw the weariness in his eyes.

"What happened?"

Removing his hat, he raked a hand through his dark hair. "A group of trail hands rode into town, already drunk as skunks and looking to raise a raucous. It took a while before me and some other deputies managed to round them up and lock them in the jail to sleep it off. They'll be facing some stiff fines for all the damage they caused."

Dorinda nodded, relief washing over her. "You must be exhausted. I'll start some coffee and wake Joel. It's not long before we should leave for the school."

After they had eaten, Dutch helped Dorinda tidy up before they headed out onto the front porch. Joel scampered down the steps, chasing after a dog trotting down the road.

As they walked past the sheriff's office, the front door banged open. Sheriff Evans hurried out, buckling on his gunbelt. His expression was grim.

"Trouble at Teddy Minor's spread," he called to Dutch as he strode toward them. "He sent his son to town. Rustlers raided their root cellar and took several head of cattle. I'm headed down there now."

Dutch's relaxed mood evaporated. His instincts were on high alert. "I'll go with you."

He turned to Dorinda, his eyes apologetic. "I have to go. I'll come by later today or tomorrow. Don't worry if you don't hear from me." He took off after Gabe.

She didn't have time to fret. Joel was her first priority. She held out her hand for Joel. "Come on, sweetheart. Let's get to school."

Joel skipped along next to her, chattering, oblivious to her concern. As they turned onto their street, a shout rang out.

"Dorinda! Wait!"

She turned to see Amelia Wheeler rushing toward her, face flushed, clutching her skirts in one hand.

"What's happened?"

"It's awful," Amelia panted. "I was just opening

the schoolhouse, and I found two of the windows smashed. Books and slates strewn everywhere. It's a mess."

Dorinda pressed a hand to her mouth in dismay. More lawlessness, just as Dutch had warned.

"Did you see who did it?"

Amelia shook her head. "No, it must have happened during the night. I wanted you to know before the children arrive."

Dorinda's mind raced, thinking of how to handle this latest challenge. "Let's check the damage and make a list of what we'll need to make repairs. We'll clean up the best we can before the children arrive."

Amelia nodded, her expression easing with relief at Dorinda's calm manner. They hurried to the schoolhouse, their focus on the day ahead. There was work to be done.

As they reached the schoolhouse, Morgan Wheeler, Amelia's husband, ran past her, his lungs burning. They looked in the direction he ran to see a fleeing boy.

"Who is he chasing?" Dorinda asked.

"I don't know." Amelia continued to stare after them.

Joel came around his mother and stopped. "I know him."

Dorinda's brows drew together. "Who is he?"

"Walter."

"Walter who?"

Joel shook his head. "I don't know. He doesn't go to school."

"Do you know who his parents are?" Dorinda prodded.

"No." He took off when he spotted boys he knew.

Leaves and twigs snapped under Morgan's boots as he darted between the trees behind the saloons and boardinghouse, focused on his quarry.

The boy wove between the trees ahead of him, glancing back now and then with wide, frightened eyes. Morgan poured on a burst of speed, his longer legs eating up the distance.

His legs burned as he continued sprinting after him down the path along the creek. The boy was quick and agile, darting between trees and jumping over bushes in an attempt to lose his pursuer. Morgan was determined not to lose this pursuit, pumping his arms and breathing heavily as he tried to close the gap.

He deftly hurdled a fallen log, never losing sight of the small figure up ahead. The boy glanced back, his eyes widening at how close the deputy had gotten.

Morgan felt a swell of triumph as he anticipated finally catching the troublesome boy. But just as he stretched out his hand, the little rascal made a sharp turn between two buildings up ahead. Adjusting direction, Morgan pushed his aching legs faster, skidding after him, only to find...nothing. The boy had vanished.

Morgan bent over, hands on his knees as he caught his breath. Frustration and disappointment coursed through him. So close, yet the boy had slipped through his grasp once again. He slammed his fist against the building in anger.

This was far from over, Morgan vowed. He would not rest until he got to the bottom of the boy's mischief. Straightening up, he strode along the boardwalk, frustration still simmering from his failure to nab the boy. He needed to regroup and think about his next move.

As he walked toward the schoolhouse, he spotted Amelia and Dorinda up ahead, talking with some of the townspeople. Their faces were creased with worry. He knew how much the teachers cared for the children.

Instead of joining them, Morgan headed toward the narrow passage between the Splendor Herald newspaper and Finn's saloon, the last place he'd seen the boy. He'd disappeared as fast as a jackrabbit down a hole. He was determined to uncover any clues as to where the boy might be hiding out.

"You looking for the boy who hightailed it out of the alleyway a bit ago?" Deputy Cash Coulter leaned against a boardwalk post, examining a small piece of wood meant for whittling.

"I'm almost sure he broke windows and upturned desks in the schoolhouse."

Cash shook his head as he straightened away from the post. "That'll be hard to prove unless he confesses or someone saw him."

"I know. Still, I want to find him."

"He dashed across Frontier Street and down the alleyway between the general store and McCall's restaurant. I'm guessing he continued between Ruby's and the houses until he reached the forest. No telling where he went from there. Let me know if you want help tracking him."

"Thanks, Cash. I just might do that."

"I'd best get on my rounds."

Morgan moved swiftly toward the western edge of town and through a field before reaching the tree line. He didn't want to startle the boy if he was hiding nearby.

He stepped into the shadows of the woods. Twigs and dry leaves crunched under his boots as he picked his way along a faint path. The trees grew denser the farther in he went. Morgan scanned the darkness, searching for any sign of the boy.

A flash of movement caught his eye. Morgan froze, peering into the brush. Had it been a squirrel darting by or something more? He waited, staying still, until he caught another flicker through the leaves up ahead. Morgan inched forward, pulse quickening.

As he peered around a large tree trunk, Morgan spotted a small clearing. There in the center, hunched on the ground against a fallen log, was the unmistakable figure of a boy. He sat with his head bowed, thin arms wrapped around his knees.

Morgan let out a slow breath, then stepped into the clearing. The boy's head jerked up, eyes wide with alarm. For a moment, they stared at each other. Then the boy leapt to his feet.

Morgan held up a hand. "It's all right, son. I'm not going to hurt you." He kept his voice low and calm. "How about we go get you something to eat?"

Hesitating, the boy glanced around as if looking for an escape route. Morgan stayed still, sensing the boy's fear.

"I know you're scared. We'll walk back into town together." He extended a hand. After a long moment, the boy stepped forward, ignoring the hand. Morgan gave him a reassuring grin.

Relief washed over him as he led the boy from the woods. Morgan kept a gentle hand on the boy's thin shoulder when they reached the edge of town. "What's your name?"

After a moment, he answered in a voice so low Morgan almost didn't hear. "Walter."

"Well, Walter, let's get you some hot food."

They walked between houses and stores until they arrived back on Frontier Street. He opened the door of McCall's, ushering Walter inside. They took a table near the kitchen.

Betts walked up. "So, who do we have here?"

"This is Walter. I don't believe he's eaten in a while," Morgan answered.

"How about I bring him a plate of eggs, potatoes, bacon, and a thick slice of bread?"

"Great, Betts. Thank you."

Walter devoured everything she brought. Morgan sat with him, keeping the conversation light. The boy's shoulders relaxed a little more with each bite.

Pushing the plate away, Walter looked up at Morgan, gifting the deputy with a cautious smile.

Chapter Three

Morgan escorted Walter from McCall's to the jail, one hand resting on the boy's slender shoulder. Though Walter had cleaned his plate of eggs, bacon, potatoes, and an extra plate of flapjacks, his stomach continued to growl, as if he hadn't eaten at all. The oversized woolen shirt he wore hung from his malnourished frame.

Sheriff Gabe Evans rose from behind his desk as Morgan led the boy inside. His keen eyes assessed Walter's condition in an instant, though his expression remained neutral.

"Morning, Sheriff," Morgan said. "This is Walter."

Gabe nodded, gesturing to a chair. "Have a seat, son."

Walter perched tentatively on the edge of the seat, eyes lowered.

"I'm Sheriff Evans," Gabe said, leaning back in his chair. "You're not in any trouble. I'd just like to ask you a few questions, if that's all right."

The boy said nothing, fingers worrying at a fray-

GHOST LAGOON

ing cuff.

"Where are your folks, Walter?" Gabe asked. When the boy didn't respond, he asked a second question. "Do you have family around here?"

Silence. The ticking of the wall clock underscored the pause.

Gabe tried again. "Folks are mighty worried about the damage to the schoolhouse. Windows were broken, desks turned over. Do you know anything about that?"

Walter's shoulders hunched inward as his lips twisted.

Gabe sighed, casting a rueful glance at Morgan. For now, it seemed, the boy's secrets would remain his own.

Gabe rubbed a hand over his stubbled chin, thinking. The boy was clearly in some kind of trouble, but getting answers would require patience and care.

"All right. We'll let it rest for now." He turned to Morgan. "Why don't you take him over to the orphanage? Maybe Martha can get through to him."

The deputy nodded. "Good idea, Sheriff. I'll take him there now."

He placed a gentle hand on Walter's shoulder. "Come on, Walter. Let's head out."

The boy allowed himself to be led outside. They headed to the schoolhouse, where he spotted his wife standing on the entrance stoop. Amelia offered Walter a kind smile.

"I'm taking Walter to Martha."

She nodded, understanding the boy had nowhere

else to go. "Deputy Wheeler is going to take you someplace safe, Walter. You'll have a bed and plenty of food to eat. Miss Martha will make sure you're well cared for, and there are other boys and girls to play with," she called after them as Morgan walked with Walter to the livery to saddle his horse.

Walter said nothing as he rode in front of Morgan on the trip to the orphanage.

A couple miles from town stood a two-story house with a whitewashed porch and dormer windows. Morgan reined his horse to a stop and dismounted.

"Here we are." He lifted Walter down, guiding him up the steps. Morgan gave the door a brisk knock.

It opened to reveal a tall, statuesque woman in a floral cotton dress. Martha Santori's soft brown eyes crinkled as she smiled at Walter.

"Hello, Deputy Wheeler. Please, come inside."

She stepped back, allowing them to enter. The foyer was humble but homey, with a braided rug and landscape paintings on the walls.

"Who do we have here?" she asked.

"This is Walter. Walter, this is Mrs. Santori."

"It's a pleasure to meet you, Walter. You may call me Miss Martha or Mrs. Santori, whichever you like. Let me show you around." She beckoned for Walter to follow. Morgan trailed behind as she led them through the various rooms.

"You'll meet the other children at supper," Martha told Walter. "I think you'll like it here. It may take some getting used to, but we're so happy to have you."

Walter studied the floor, shoulders hunched. But he hadn't resisted coming inside. It was a start. Martha led Walter upstairs to a long room lined with neat beds. She gestured to one in the corner.

"This will be your bed," she said. "Why don't you have a seat and get comfortable?"

Walter perched tentatively on the edge of the mattress. Martha handed him a canvas bag.

"There's a fresh set of clothes in here, and a few other things you'll need." She smiled. "Make yourself at home. I know this is all new, but you're safe here."

Walter nodded, clutching the bag to his chest.

"We'll let you get settled." Martha turned to Morgan. "Would you care for some tea before you head back?"

"Thank you, but I need to get back," said Morgan. "Walter, if you ever need me, ask Miss Martha to send someone to town. You already met my wife, Miss Amelia. She and I ride out on Sundays, so you'll see me at least once a week." He turned to leave, stopping when Walter jumped from the bed to clutch Morgan's pants with his small hand. Looking up at the deputy, his eyes began to tear.

"I want to go with you."

Morgan knelt in front of him. "Miss Martha is going to take real good care of you. And I promise, there are children here who will become your friends."

Walter's arms flew around Morgan's neck, desperate to keep him from leaving. After a moment,

Martha removed his thin arms and took one of his hands in hers.

"Why don't we go outside and meet some of the other children, Walter."

Staring back at Morgan, he held his gaze. "Sunday..."

"Yes, Walter. I will see you on Sunday."

A few minutes later, Martha joined him in her office. "Can you tell me anything more about him?"

"Wish I could. We only have his first name. He refused to answer any questions from Gabe or me. There's a chance some of the children at the school know him. Or some of the orphans who attend school in town."

"I'll ask the children after supper. We sure do miss Amelia around here. The new woman, Betsy, is real sweet and is a fine cook, but she's not Amelia."

Morgan turned to leave. "We'll be out on Sunday. Get word to me if..."

Martha walked up to him, placing a hand on his arm. "You did the right thing bringing him here. I remember when Dutch brought Wilma and Harry to the orphanage. There was a moment when I thought that big, strong deputy was going to cry."

He nodded, blinking away moisture in his eyes. "Yes, ma'am."

"We'll look forward to seeing you and Amelia on Sunday."

"Thank you, ma'am."

"Travel safely." Martha walked him onto the porch. As he rode away, she peered up at the dormer windows, hoping in her heart Walter would find peace within these walls.

Two days later, Dorinda called the children inside for the final lesson of the day. Counting, her brow furrowed with concern. She hadn't seen Joel.

Closing the door, her gaze moved over the classroom. Her chest tightened in fear when realizing her son wasn't inside.

"What is it?" Amelia asked.

Dorinda shook her head. "Joel didn't come back inside. I need to search the grounds."

"Go on. I'll ask the children if they know where Joel went."

Dorinda felt her heart drop. Dashing outside, she hurried around the schoolhouse, calling his name over and over. Running to the creek, she looked up and down the water's edge. Checking around and under bushes, she straightened, telling herself not to panic.

Heading back into the schoolhouse, she saw the look on Amelia's face and the slight shake of her head. No one knew where Joel had gone.

"I'll go alert the sheriff," Amelia said, already heading for the door.

Dorinda nodded, her mind racing. She began counting heads for the third time, ensuring all the other children were accounted for. As she did, dread crept up her spine. What if something horrible had happened to her son? Her stomach lurched in a violent cramp, bending her over.

One of the older girls raced to her. "Are you all right, Miss Dorinda? Should I get the doctor?"

"No, no. I'm fine. Worried about where Joel got off to."

The girl nodded. "He was playing, then he was just...gone."

Amelia raced across Frontier Street and onto the boardwalk. Bursting through the door of Gabe's office, she quickly explained the situation. She'd hoped to find Morgan inside. Instead, Dutch stood from where he'd been sitting, drinking a cup of coffee.

"Did you look everywhere?" Dutch asked.

"Dorinda searched outside, calling for him. We counted the children at least three times, and no one else is missing. And no one saw him leave the school area."

"I'll gather some deputies and we'll start searching the town," Gabe said. "He can't have gone far."

Soon enough, Gabe, Dutch, Morgan, and most of the other deputies were searching the town and wooded areas surrounding the perimeter of Splendor. They coordinated with other townsfolk to cover as much ground as possible, hoping to find Joel before darkness fell. As the afternoon wore on without any sign of the boy, a pall of worry settled over the town.

Gabe wiped sweat from his brow as the sun sank lower in the sky. They'd been searching the land in every direction for hours to no avail. Joel was still missing.

"Let's head back into town and regroup," he told Morgan and Dutch. "Maybe someone else found Joel. If not, we'll start again at first light."

The three men turned their horses toward Splendor, defeat weighing heavy on their shoulders. When they arrived back in town, a small crowd had gathered. Friends and neighbors looked to Gabe expectantly, but he could only shake his head.

A cry went up from Dorinda as she collapsed into Amelia's arms. The disappearance of her son was almost too much for her to bear.

Dismounting, Dutch hurried to her. "We'll find him, Dorinda," he said, though his reassuring words felt hollow. In his gut, he knew the chances of locating Joel alive and unharmed were slim. Still, he couldn't bring himself to voice the bleak thought.

"I want every able-bodied person up at dawn ready to join the search," Gabe announced to the crowd. A chorus of solemn agreement followed.

As darkness fell over Splendor, an air of uncertainty and dread settled over the town. Joel was still missing, and the outcome was far from certain. Dutch stared up at the night sky, hoping tomorrow would bring answers. With Joel's life hanging in the balance, he knew no one would rest easy tonight.

Dutch placed a comforting hand on Dorinda's shoulder. "We'll find him. I won't rest until we do." Though they'd searched all day to no avail, Dutch wouldn't allow uncertainty or despair to weaken his resolve.

She lifted her tear-stained face. "My boy is out there, scared and alone. You have to bring him home."

"We will do everything possible to find him," Dutch replied. Looking into Dorinda's anguished eyes, he made a silent vow not to stop until Joel was safe.

Gabe strode over, his expression grim. "I've asked several deputies to keep searching through the night in case..." His voice trailed off, not wanting to give voice to the terrible possibilities.

"I'll take the north quadrant," Dutch offered.

Gabe nodded. "There are also some townsfolk who'll keep searching. Noah, Nick, Sean MacLaren, and several others. I'm thinking of sending a rider to the Pelletier ranch. Dax and Luke would be happy to help out." Though exhausted from the day's efforts, neither man was willing to rest with Joel still missing.

"I can ride out," Morgan offered.

"I'll go," Dutch said.

"No, you stay in town, close to Dorinda," Gabe said. "Go ahead and ride out, Morgan. Take Tucker or Jonas with you." Gabe mentioned fellow deputies and Morgan's closest friends.

As Morgan headed out to locate Tucker or Jonas, his thoughts turned to Amelia. Her strength and compassion had shone through as she'd comforted Dorinda.

Finding Tucker, they mounted up and rode into the deepening night. He couldn't image what Dorinda was feeling. The devastated look on her face said so much more than a few strained words. He felt the same as Dutch. No matter how long it took, they'd continue to search until Joel was safely back with his mother.

Chapter Four

Morgan, Tucker, Jonas, and Dutch spread out a little before dawn the following morning. They'd been given the area east of Splendor, between the town and the MacLaren ranch. Morgan and Dutch believed Joel had either walked or been taken in this direction.

Jonas and Tucker weren't as sure. All four deputies believed Joel was still alive. They also believed it critical he was found within the next two days.

They called out Joel's name, straining to hear any cry for help over the sounds of the emerging day. As the hours wore on, doubt began to creep into their minds. What if they didn't find the boy out here? Then they'd believe another group searching the other areas would locate him.

Up ahead, Dutch spotted the cabin owned by Widow Ida. Some called her Old Ida. She answered to either name, always appreciative when anyone stopped by to chat.

Reining his horse to the side of the cabin, he dismounted. Taking a moment to stretch his taut

GHOST LAGOON

muscles, he strode to the door and pounded.

"Ida, it's Dutch McFarlin. Are you in there?" He waited, hearing someone shuffling about. The door opened on a slender woman close to seventy with sparse, white hair, gaunt features, and weathered hands. She wore men's pants, an oversized shirt, and boots which had to be twenty or thirty years old.

"Dutch. Come in." Drawing the door wide. "What brings you out this way?"

"A boy's missing."

"Missing or taken?" A fare question given the times.

"We don't know. He was in the schoolyard with the other children, but didn't return inside. His mother is one of the teachers. We've been searching since yesterday."

She lowered herself into a threadbare chair, waving her arm for him to do the same. "You want to know if I've seen anything?"

"I do."

"You're the first person to come this way since those MacLaren brothers stopped on their way to town a week ago. Real nice boys. They stopped on their way back to their ranch to give me some items from the general store and meat market. I sure appreciate them."

"No sign of anyone else?"

She shook her head.

"Hear anything?"

"Usual coyotes, owls, and such."

Nodding, he pushed himself up from the too small

37

chair. She stood along with him.

"I'll hitch up the wagon and let Gabe know if I see anyone. Don't want any young'un getting lost out this way."

"Appreciate it, Ida. I best be on my way."

"You stay safe yourself, Dutch. Never know who's waiting up ahead to do you harm."

His mouth twitched as he touched the brim of his hat. "Good advice."

Mounting, he continued heading east, calling Joel's name. His hope the boy would be out this direction faded with each mile. He met up with the others mid-afternoon.

"I'd say we circle back the way we came," Jonas said. "We might spot something we didn't see the first time."

Taking Jonas's suggestion, they headed back to town, a noticeable pall changing the mood from when they'd started all those hours ago.

Dutch dreaded telling Dorinda they had nothing to show for all the hours in the saddle. He hated offering a woman he cared about little hope her son would return. All he could provide were more hours of searching tomorrow, the next day, and the day following.

Riding into town, the bleak expressions on the four faces signaled louder than words their lack of success. Stopping at the jail, they dismounted, exhausted from long hours in the saddle. Finding the jail empty, they crossed the street to the Dixie.

Even the popular saloon lacked the usual late

afternoon crowd. As they settled at a table, a loud shout joined by several more loud voices filtered into the saloon.

Shoving back their chairs, the four dashed out the swinging doors to the boardwalk. People were running toward the schoolhouse, some wearing broad smiles.

Dutch began walking. "We'd best go see what everyone's so excited about."

It didn't take long to spot what had everyone so fired up. Joel, tired looking and wearing clothes dirty and torn, stood next to Dorinda. Tears streamed down her face as she wrapped her arms around her son. The deputies circled around Gabe.

"Who found him?" Dutch asked.

"No one. He showed up at the school a little bit ago. Bernie Griggs at the telegraph office saw him and rushed to the school, shouting as he ran. Dorinda and Amelia were inside and heard the commotion."

"They came outside to find Joel," Dutch said.

"No one has questioned him yet. I hope Dorinda doesn't put up a fuss about discovering where he's been all these hours." Gabe's jaw tightened, watching the boy hug his mother.

"I'll talk to her."

"Thanks, Dutch. Let me know what you learn." Gabe turned to the other deputies. "Make a thorough search of the area around the school. Get Cash Coulter to go with you."

"What are we looking for, Gabe?"

"Tracks and anything that doesn't fit," the sheriff

answered. "There's a good chance someone took Joel and brought him back. Nothing else makes sense."

"Who would do such a thing?" Tucker asked.

"I don't know. But someone did. I'm going back to the jail."

The deputies watched him leave before circling up to do what Gabe ordered.

"I agree with Gabe. I'm going to talk to Joel and Dorinda," Dutch said.

Morgan set a hand on his shoulder. "Hope you learn something."

"So do I."

Dutch sat in Dorinda's living room, watching Joel, who sat at the kitchen table, staring at a bowl of stew. He hadn't said a word to anyone since Bernie had found him outside the school.

"I don't know what to do." Dorinda took a seat near Dutch on the sofa. "Not one word. He looks at the ground, but won't look at me." She swiped at another round of tears rolling down her face.

Squeezing her arm, he stood, crossing the distance to the table in a few steps. He sat down, keeping his body relaxed, his words friendly.

"We sure did miss you, Joel. The whole town was worried about you. In all my years as a lawman, I've never seen so many people volunteer to search."

Joel glanced up for a second before returning his

attention to the now cold bowl of stew.

"I don't think you wandered off, son. My guess is you saw someone you knew and went to see if you were right. Am I close?"

Again, Joel lifted his gaze. At that instant, Dutch knew he was right.

"I'm also guessing you were so glad to see the person, you took off without thinking about your mother or school or anything else. Does that sound about right?"

Joel's jaw worked before his throat constricted in a spontaneous swallow, but he didn't look up. Picking up a spoon, he stirred the stew without taking a bite.

"Your food must be cold. Do you want me to warm it up for you?"

Dropping the spoon, he clasped his hands in his lap. Joel stared at something on a wall in front of him, refusing to let Dutch drag him into a conversation. Without a word, he slid from the chair, glanced at Dorinda, then walked into the bedroom, closing the door behind him.

Sighing, Dutch returned to the sofa, lowering himself next to Dorinda. "He needs some time. He'll talk about where he's been after some rest. Be patient. You may want to have one of the doctors check him out."

"Yes. I was thinking the same."

"Do you want me to stay for a while?"

Releasing a sigh, she shook her head. "You've had a long day. I appreciate you coming to the house and trying to get Joel to talk." She stood and walked to the door. "Go home and get some rest."

When he reached her, he swept hair from her face before dropping his hand. "You do the same. And don't worry. He'll talk when he's ready."

On the walk to the jail, he thought about what he'd said to Dorinda. Dutch wasn't at all sure Joel would talk any time soon.

"All right. It's time to break into your groups. You'll be working on your numbers today." Dorinda let out a breath, taking a quick glance at Joel.

It had been days since he'd returned to the school, and had yet to utter a word about his disappearance. At least he wasn't totally silent, as he'd been the first twenty-four hours. Joel answered questions directed to him at school, used please and thank you, and said goodnight when Dorinda tucked him in bed for the night.

Still, something wasn't quite right. She'd find him staring into the distance, as if searching for someone. His smiles were few, and his laughter silent.

It gratified Dorinda to find he still had the same, strong appetite. For a boy of six, he could eat as much as a young man.

"Does everyone have their slates and slate pencils?" Dorinda asked.

"Yes, Miss Dorinda," the class responded.

"Wonderful. Miss Amelia is writing the problems

on the front board. Please use your slate and slate pencils to solve them. Work together. Raise your hand if you have a question."

She walked over to where Amelia stood. For the last two days, Amelia had volunteered to work with Joel, hoping to get him to talk about the time he was away. He'd always had a special relationship with her, confiding what bothered him when he wouldn't tell Dorinda. Both women hoped he'd do the same now. So far, Joel had kept everything locked tight inside him.

After school today, they were going for a ride with Dutch. Not in a wagon this time. Dutch had arranged with Noah Brandt, the owner of the livery and Gabe Evans's best friend since they were children in New York, to saddle two additional horses.

Joel loved horses and had no idea what was planned. She couldn't wait to see his response.

At three o'clock, the women excused the children for the day. Dorinda made sure Joel had his hat and coat before leaving. It would be chilly before they returned from the ride.

"Are you hungry?"

"No, thank you."

Instead of Dorinda taking the normal route to the general store, meat market, then home, she turned a corner to face the livery and stables. Dutch stood outside next to three horses.

Joel's face showed surprise, though he remained silent. His pace increased until he almost ran toward Dutch.

"Are these yours?" Joel pointed at the other two horses.

"They belong to Mr. Brandt. I made an arrangement with him to use them today."

Joel looked between Dutch and his mother. "For what?"

"I thought we'd go for a ride. What do you think?"

A huge smile grew on Joel's face. "Yes!"

Chapter Five

The horses danced in place as Dutch helped Joel into the saddle of a small, black gelding. The boy wriggled to get comfortable, gripping the horn with both hands.

"The horse will sense if you're nervous, Joel. Relax and let your body move with his."

Joel nodded, inhaling and exhaling deep breaths.

Dutch patted the horse's neck before moving to aid Dorinda. She placed her foot in his cupped hands and pulled herself up and into the saddle with practiced ease.

"Excellent. All set?" Dutch asked.

"Yes, thank you," Dorinda replied, adjusting her skirt.

Dutch swung up onto his own mount, a tall bay gelding. "Joel, are you ready?"

Nodding eagerly, he gripped the reins.

"Let's go."

Dutch led them from the livery onto a narrow trail winding its way up into the tall pines of the foothills.

Sunlight filtered through the trees and onto the well-worn trail.

Joel craned his neck, taking in the scenery. His original tight grip on the reins began to loosen. A hint of a smile crossed his lips.

As they rode, Dutch kept one eye on the trail ahead and one on Joel.

"Try moving with him," he suggested. "Rise and fall with each step."

Joel nodded, bouncing awkwardly at first before finding the rhythm. His shoulders loosened.

"That's it," Dutch said. "You're a natural."

Joel grinned, sitting taller in the saddle. Gripping the saddlehorn, he leaned forward, giving the horse an appreciative pat on the neck.

Dutch began pointing out wildlife along the way, such as a jackrabbit dashing across the trail in front of them and a red-tailed hawk circling overhead. Joel listened, his eyes bright with curiosity.

It didn't take long before they came upon Dutch's destination. A glistening pond, surrounded by lush bushes and trees, beckoned them. Reining in, Dutch dismounted before helping Dorinda and Joel slide from their saddles, their boots sinking into the muddy bank.

Spying a frog, he rushed around the pond to where it stood on the edge of the water. Crouching down, he scooped it up, laughing.

"Mama, look!" He held it out for her inspection.

Dorinda smiled at the joyful sound of her son's laughter. It had been too long since she'd heard it.

She met Dutch's gaze over Joel's head, gratitude shining in her eyes.

Joel played with the frog for quite a while before releasing it beside the lagoon. Joel scampered along the water's edge, peering past the ripples in search of more wildlife. He let out a whoop as a fish darted by, its silver scales glinting.

Dutch tethered their horses between two trees before retrieving two bundles from his saddlebag and the rolled blanket behind the saddle. His stomach rumbled at the aroma escaping into the air.

Approaching the open area where Dorinda watched Joel, he dropped the blanket on the ground. She whirled at the sound.

"Thought we could use a little picnic," he said.

"How wonderful, Dutch. I'll spread the blanket out."

When she finished, he set the bundles on the blanket. Dorinda began pulling the food out, her stomach growling along with Dutch's. Joel ran over to peer into the canvas bags.

His eyes went wide at the sight of fried chicken, biscuits, jam, and oatmeal cookies. He wasted no time digging in.

She watched her son eat with a joy she hadn't seen in a while. Accepting a biscuit from Dutch, she held it in her hand.

"This was real kind of you," she said, taking a bite of the biscuit.

He gave a modest shrug. "After being cooped up so long, the boy needed some space from the townsfolk watching him."

They ate in contented silence for a spell, Joel finishing first. Jumping up, he rushed off to explore. Dorinda's expression turned solemn as she studied her son. There was still so much he wasn't saying about his ordeal. She worried about what scars remained beneath the surface.

Dutch seemed to read her thoughts. "Give him time. He'll open up when he's ready."

She nodded, though an unease lingered in her heart. She glanced westward, where the sun was slipping behind the mountains.

"Best to head back before dark," Dutch said, rising to gather their things.

Dorinda nodded in agreement as they mounted their horses again. She was thankful for this brief respite from the troubles that plagued them. She hoped Joel would someday find the courage to share his story. For now, she was grateful for this small step toward healing.

As they turned back toward town, she noticed Joel looking over his shoulder at the pond. She knew their excursion had brought him joy and lifted his spirits.

Riding alongside her, Dutch noticed the worry on her face and repeated the sentiment he'd shared earlier. "He's a strong kid. He'll come around when he's ready."

Dorinda sighed. "I hope you're right. I just want to help him, but I don't know how."

"You're already helping more than you know," Dutch said.

Comforted by his words, Dorinda felt a swell of gratitude for this kind man who had shown such compassion for her boy.

As they approached the outskirts of Splendor, Dorinda glanced over at Joel, pleased at the smile on his face. The afternoon's outing had brought a lightness to all of them.

Reaching the livery, they dismounted. "I'll take care of the saddles, Dorinda. If you have time to wait, I'll walk you home."

He began unsaddling the horses. Joel approached, looking up at Dutch with shy admiration. "Thank you for taking us to the pond."

His eyes crinkled. "You're quite welcome, son." He ruffled the boy's hair. "Maybe we can go again sometime. I'll teach you how to fish."

Joel's face glowed with excitement. "I'd like that."

After taking care of the horses, they began the walk to Dorinda's house. "I can't thank you enough. You've given him a precious gift today."

He chuckled. "I enjoyed the time away, myself."

Dorinda smiled up at him. "So did I."

Joel skipped to his mother, taking her hand as they approached the house. She was reluctant to end this day, knowing the darkness would bring back her worries and Joel's nightmares.

"Why don't you stay for supper, Dutch? There's plenty of stew."

He hesitated, then nodded. "I'd like that."

The boy looked up at his mother. "Can we have biscuits?"

"As many as you can eat." She chuckled.

When they entered the house, Dutch headed to the stove in the kitchen to stoke the embers. He then did the same to the stoves in the living room and bedroom. Dorinda helped Joel wash up. It wasn't long before they were gathered around the scrubbed pine table, passing bowls of stew, biscuits, and preserves.

Joel devoured three biscuits, laughing when Dutch teased him about leaving room for dessert. The sound of the boy's laughter lifted her spirits. Joel seemed unburdened, like the child he was before his disappearance.

After a slice of pie, he grew drowsy. She settled him in the bed, covering him with a quilt. Dorinda returned to the table, where Dutch sat drinking coffee. They spoke in hushed tones about the day, about taking another ride in the future.

Morning sunlight streamed through the bedroom curtains, rousing Dorinda from a fitful sleep. She blinked open her eyes to see Joel still curled up beside her, his small frame rising and falling with steady breaths. Careful not to wake him, she slipped from the bed and tucked the quilts snugly around his shoulders.

After washing up and slipping into clean clothes, Dorinda tidied the room and set out a fresh set of clothes for Joel. She would let him sleep a while longer while she fixed breakfast. Her stomach rumbled, but food could wait.

A knock at the door made her jump. She crossed the living room and opened it a crack to see Morgan standing there, hat in hand.

"Morning, Dorinda. I was hoping to have a word with you and Joel if you have a moment."

She stepped onto the porch. "Let's speak out here. Joel's still asleep."

He nodded, an apologetic look in his eyes. "I know it's early, but the sheriff wanted me to come by and ask if Joel remembered anything else that could help us figure out what went on that day."

"I'm afraid not. He slept through the night for the first time since..." Her voice trailed off for a moment. "Joel's been having nightmares."

Morgan sighed. "We'll keep trying to figure it out. I know it's hard on both of you, but we need Joel to try and open up when he's ready."

The door creaked open wider behind Dorinda. She turned to see Joel peering up at them, clutching his blanket.

"Is it time for breakfast?" he mumbled.

Dorinda glanced uncertainly at Morgan. Perhaps it was best to start this difficult conversation before Joel was fully awake. She knelt down and took her son's hands.

"Sweetheart, Deputy Wheeler needs to ask you some questions first, about when you went away. I know it's scary to remember, but can you try your

SHIRLEEN DAVIES

best?"

Joel's face clouded. He shrank back against the doorframe.

"I don't want to."

Dorinda exchanged a pained look with Morgan. They couldn't force Joel to relive his ordeal. But the search for answers couldn't end here.

"All right, Joel. Go wash up. I set out clean clothes for you. I'll get your breakfast started."

He rushed back into the bedroom, closing the door.

"Sorry, Dorinda. I'll let the sheriff know he's not ready to talk. At least we tried."

"Thank you, Morgan." Closing the door, she rested her back against it, wondering when all the guessing would go away, and they'd finally have some answers.

Chapter Six

Dutch stood motionless, staring at the telegram in his hand. The words blurred together as his mind reeled. *Your parents, struggling. The estate, falling into disrepair.* It couldn't be true, but Mr. Carlson's brief message and dire tone left no room for doubt.

With a deep breath, Dutch read over the telegram again, hoping he'd misunderstood. The meaning remained unchanged. His shoulders slumped, and a hollow feeling settled in his gut. After everything his family had weathered, could the message signal the end of his family's legacy?

He recalled his stately childhood home, once filled with light and laughter. The sprawling porches where he'd sat with his older brother, dreaming of the future. The winding garden paths where he and Lowell invented grand adventures. The home had been in his family for years. To imagine its decline was hard to conceive.

Dutch pushed open the door to the telegraph office, the bell above the door announcing his arrival.

Bernie Griggs looked up from behind the counter, his spectacles perched on the end of his nose.

"Afternoon, Deputy," Bernie said. "Did you get the telegram I left for you at the jail?"

Dutch stepped to the counter. "I did. That's why I'm here. I need to send a reply telegram right away. It's urgent."

Bernie nodded several times, his fingers drumming on the counter. "Do you want to fill this out, or tell me what you want to say?"

"You go ahead, Bernie. It goes to Mr. Hiram Carlson in Charleston, South Carolina. He's a neighbor of my folks," Dutch said.

Bernie wrote in his small print. "What do you want to say, Deputy?"

"Appreciate information. Concerned about parents and estate. Will contact banker to learn more."

Bernie finished transcribing the message. "How do you want it signed, Deputy?"

"Just with Dutch."

Bouncing on the balls of his feet, Bernie counted the words, giving him the fee. Reaching into a pocket, Dutch set money on the counter.

"Appreciate it, Bernie."

"Sure thing, Deputy. I'll get this right out for you."

Dutch stepped back outside into the afternoon sun. He needed time to think, to process this news about his family. Tipping his hat to the passersby, he set off down the crowded boardwalk.

He nodded in greeting to Stan Petermann, owner of the general store. Stan paused in sweeping the boardwalk in front of his store. "Afternoon, Deputy. Everything all right?" he asked, noting the furrow in Dutch's brow.

"Well enough, Stan, thank you," Dutch replied. He kept walking, immersed in thought.

Up ahead, he came upon Nick Barnett as he exited the Dixie. "Dutch." The men shook hands. "You doing all right?"

"Been better."

"Come on in the Dixie. I'll buy you a drink."

Dutch managed a faint smile. "Appreciate the offer, Nick. Another time." With a parting tip of his hat, he continued on.

Nick watched the deputy's retreating figure, a flicker of concern in his eyes. It wasn't like Dutch to refuse a drink at the end of the day. Shaking his head, Nick went back to his office in the back of the Dixie.

Dutch walked on, barely noticing the sights and sounds of town. His mind was filled with memories of better times and worries for the future.

He pictured his family's grand Victorian house, with its wide porches and sprawling gardens. Lowell loved playing hide and seek with Dutch amid the sculpted hedges, darting down brick pathways and secret alcoves. Laughter echoed through those gardens, filling their days with joy and mischief.

Other memories surfaced, too. All the lazy summer afternoons he'd spent fishing off the dock, fireflies dancing in the dusk while he and Lowell whispered plans and dreams, the family enjoying a quiet evening on the veranda.

Most of all, Dutch remembered his bond with Lowell. His brother had been his staunchest friend and ally, always ready for their next grand adventure. How they had dreamed together, conspiring to build a boat to sail the seas. Lowell made him feel the two of them could do anything.

The image of his brother now brought an ache to Dutch's heart. Losing Lowell to the war against the Union had left a void no one could fill. He was thankful the love they shared endured, guiding Dutch still.

With a heavy sigh, he turned toward the house he called home.

Dutch warmed chicken stew in the oven while sipping coffee at his table. The telegram from his parents' neighbor weighed on him. Something had to be wrong with their health if they allowed the house to go into disrepair.

Ladling stew into a bowl, he refilled his coffee cup and began eating his supper. Several minutes passed before his thoughts returned to his parents and Lowell.

So much had changed after his brother's death during a battle hundreds of miles from Charleston. Dutch's heart grew heavy recalling the day he'd received word of Lowell's death. He'd been stationed in Richmond, Virginia, as part of the Confederate

Secret Service, when the telegram arrived. Short and terse, it stated his brother had fallen in battle.

At first, he refused to believe it, certain there'd been some mistake. Lowell could not be gone, he'd told himself. His brother was too full of life and promise.

As the weeks passed with no further word, the awful truth sank in. Dutch would never again hear Lowell's laughter or see his infectious grin. All plans and dreams they'd conceived together, died with his brother. The war had stolen so much, but taking Lowell was the cruelest blow of all.

For a long time after his death, Dutch had been swamped in grief. Eventually, he realized Lowell would not want him to give up. His brother had always inspired him to keep fighting for what was right.

After the South conceded defeat, and against the odds, Union supporter Allan Pinkerton had hired Dutch as one of his agents. He'd poured his pain into the assignments, seeking justice for others.

Now, facing fresh trials with his family, Dutch drew on Lowell's memory once more. His brother had taught him resilience and perseverance. Lowell lived on through him, lending him courage. Gripped by bittersweet nostalgia, Dutch placed his empty bowl in the sink and swallowed the last of his coffee.

Telling himself the time had come to move away from thoughts of Lowell, he removed his boots and stretched out on his bed. He placed his hands behind his head and stared at the ceiling.

Tomorrow morning, he'd return to the telegraph office and send a message to the family banker. Maybe he could provide answers he was desperate to read.

Dutch strode into the telegraph office the instant it opened the following morning, the bell on the door announcing his presence. Bernie looked up from his paperwork, raising an eyebrow at the deputy's intense expression.

"I need to send another wire to Charleston. It'll go to my father's banker, Arthur Pembrook."

He scribbled out a message.

Need full state of family affairs. Advise on ledgers and accounts. Concerned for parents' health. Awaiting your swift reply. D. McFarlin

Dutch slid the paper to Bernie. "Make sure this goes out straight away."

"You bet, Deputy. It'll go right out." Bernie tapped out the message.

With the telegraph on its way, Dutch stepped back onto the boardwalk into a gloomy morning. His heart felt as heavy as the dark clouds about to bust loose over the town. He still had more questions than answers about his family's situation.

Squaring his shoulders, Dutch walked to the sheriff's office to resume his duties. He nodded in greeting to the few townspeople he passed, keeping his turbulent emotions in check.

Underneath his cool exterior, Dutch's mind churned with concern. He needed answers...fast.

Dark clouds had opened up, dropping torrential rain on the town and surrounding ranches. He'd waited until they drifted north before heading to the livery. The familiar scents of hay and leather brought him a small measure of comfort. He nodded in greeting to Noah Brandt, the proprietor, as he walked back to check on his bay gelding.

As he brushed the horse's coat, Dutch's mind continued to churn with worries about his parents and the Charleston estate. He hadn't heard back from the neighbor or the family banker.

Dutch knew his father was proud to a fault and unlikely to ask for help, even if they desperately needed it. And his mother was so protective of appearances, she'd rather starve than let Charleston society see her falter.

Dutch shook his head. He wished Lowell were still here. His levelheaded brother always knew what to do in difficult situations. Yet, if Lowell had lived, Dutch wouldn't be living in Splendor. He'd be in Charleston.

After ensuring his horse was fed and settled for the night, Dutch headed toward his house. He considered stopping by Dorinda's, but his mood was too sour and self-absorbed to be around anyone.

Walking slowly, Dutch let his gaze linger on the familiar storefronts and welcoming faces of Splendor. This town had become his home, and the folks here his new family. He cared about them and took his role as deputy seriously.

As much as Charleston still held a piece of his heart, it was time for the next chapter of his life. Whatever news came, Dutch knew he could handle it. Even if he had to travel back to South Carolina to help his parents and deal with the family home, no matter how long it took, he'd return to Splendor.

With the last light fading from the sky, Dutch made the last turn toward his house. A small smile teased his lips as he recalled the sprawling flower beds and live oak trees of the family property.

He pictured his mother in her lace gloves, greeting guests on the veranda, his father, pipe in hand, strolling the manicured lawns. It was a welcome memory as he entered his empty house.

Dutch headed for the kitchen to stoke the fire and make coffee. He unpinned his deputy badge and placed it on the kitchen table.

An hour later, stomach full, he lay down, fully clothed, atop the thin mattress. Sleep would be elusive tonight with Charleston weighing so heavily on his mind.

Chapter Seven

Dorinda stood at the large slate board at the front of the classroom, slate pencil in hand, writing the day's lessons in elegant cursive. Her steady strokes filled the board. Joel sat at his desk, engrossed in a book, glancing up at his mother a few times.

The door opened, and Amelia slipped into the room a little earlier than usual. Making her way to her own desk, she overheard hushed voices from the back corner where the older students normally gathered before class.

They were speaking about the new owners of the Splendor Herald, a Mr. and Mrs. Kelly. Amelia's curiosity was piqued. She strained to hear more of their conversation until the students noticed her arrival and quieted.

Still, she wondered what changes could be in store for the resurrected town newspaper under new leadership. She resolved to keep her ears open for any other morsels of information about the new owners.

Dorinda finished writing the last lesson on the

chalkboard and turned to greet Amelia.

"Good morning."

"Good morning. I'm going to get started on preparing the geography lesson for this afternoon. How are you today?"

"Oh, I'm well. You?"

"I'm fine. Are you ready for me to ring the bell for the children?"

"Yes, I am."

Amelia walked outside to ring the school bell, signaling the start of the school day.

The morning lessons rushed by. Before long, the teachers excused the children for lunch.

Dorinda and Amelia gathered their baskets and headed outside into the early afternoon sun. They sat together in a shady spot under a tree, enjoying the light breeze.

As they ate, Amelia mentioned the conversation she'd overheard that morning about the new newspaper owners.

"It seems the students are quite curious about what changes could come with new leadership at the Herald," she remarked. "I must admit, I'm rather interested myself to see what direction they'll take things."

Dorinda nodded as she finished chewing a bite of bread. "Yes, it will be interesting to see how they put their mark on the paper. I imagine some of the older students will have some thoughts on what they'd like to read in the Herald."

"Have you spoken with Dutch lately?"

The change of subject had Dorinda setting her slice of bread down. "Not in several days. Why?"

"Morgan mentioned Dutch has been in a mood ever since getting a telegram from Charleston."

"He's from South Carolina." Dorinda wondered about what news he'd received.

"Yes, Morgan told me."

"I'll make a point of seeking him out."

Finishing their lunch, Amelia rang the bell again, calling the students back inside. As they returned to the classroom, Dorinda joined the older students for their reading lesson while Amelia met with the younger group.

"Before we begin reading today," Dorinda addressed the students, "I understand there was some talk this morning about the new owners of the Splendor Herald."

The students looked at each other, excitement sparking between them.

"I'd suggest having a discussion about what kind of news you'd like to read in the paper." Dorinda looked at each student. "What ideas do you have for making the Herald appealing and engaging for our town?"

A lively discussion ensued, the students talking in excited voices as they shared their thoughts and suggestions for the changed newspaper. Dorinda smiled as she listened to the ideas flowing from the students.

"I think it would be interesting to have more stories about the people who live here," offered one student.

"Yes," another agreed. "Something about what jobs they have, or how they spend their time outside of work."

Several students murmured in agreement.

"I'd like to read about local business owners," another student proposed. "Find out how they got started and built up their shops."

"Ask where they got the money to start a business," a male student suggested.

"I'm curious about all the new people moving into Splendor. An article about the newcomers and why they chose Splendor could be interesting," a shy girl who rarely spoke offered.

One of the most outgoing girls rushed on. "Oh, I know. What if we wrote our own column for the Herald? A place where we share stories or give our opinions each week."

This last idea generated real excitement among the group.

"We could take turns writing articles about what's happening here in town and at the ranches and farms," someone else suggested.

"I'd love to try writing something for the newspaper," a shy girl added. "Even if it was just a small piece."

The students' enthusiasm grew as they discussed the possibility of contributing their own writing to the Splendor Herald. The thrill of seeing their words and ideas published, however small, made them feel more invested in the newspaper and their own education.

Dorinda smiled as she listened to the students brainstorm different article topics, ranging from current events to personal stories. Their engagement proved this was an opportunity to channel their energy into productive work.

"Let's take some time to write down all these wonderful ideas on your slate boards," Dorinda said. "It may be possible to meet with Mr. and Mrs. Kelly and share your ideas for articles you'd be interested in writing for the Herald."

The students got to work scribbling down notes, the classroom abuzz with lively chatter about their hopes for providing articles for the newspaper.

Dorinda walked around the group, glancing over the students' shoulders to see the diverse range of article topics they were proposing. Some students focused on local events and stories, such as writing profiles of different townspeople or businesses.

Others suggested more personal perspectives, such as sharing funny anecdotes from their daily lives on the ranch or in town. A few students dreamed up serial stories they could write in installments week after week, captivating readers with thrilling tales of adventure.

As Dorinda reviewed their ideas, she was impressed by the students' creativity. Though apprehensive at first about meeting with the newspaper owners, the students now seemed eager to present their suggestions, their nervousness replaced by growing excitement.

"These are wonderful ideas, everyone." Dorinda watched as the students finished writing. "You've all put so much thought into the kinds of articles you'd like to contribute. I'm sure Mr. and Mrs. Kelly will be very impressed with all your hard work," Dorinda continued. "Now, we'll need to choose representatives to join me in presenting these ideas when we meet the owners."

The students buzzed, all hoping to be the ones selected to share their vision for a student column. Their anticipation was palpable, this opportunity filling them with a sense of purpose.

Most of the students in the group volunteered to be a representative, raising their hands and calling out. Dorinda smiled as she looked over the eager faces, knowing they all wanted to be chosen.

"Why don't all of you be part of the group?" Dorinda asked.

The students voiced their enthusiastic support. She was touched by how the group had come together, unified in this goal. She hoped the newspaper owners would recognize their enthusiasm and agree to a meeting.

"I'll speak to Mr. and Mrs. Kelly this afternoon and ask about a meeting." Dorinda noted the students' enthusiastic nods. "In the meantime, start thinking about what articles each of you wants to write for the newspaper."

The students continued to write, buzzing with anticipation as they discussed potential article topics. The classroom brimmed with creative energy.

The next morning, Dorinda gathered the group to give them the good news. "Mr. and Mrs. Kelly have agreed to meet with us today after school." She could see the nervous excitement on their faces at the opportunity to meet with the newspaper owners and pitch their idea for a student column. "Are all of you able to join me?"

Everyone nodded except for one boy. He hesitated a moment before catching Dorinda looking at him. "My pa isn't too happy if I'm not home right after school."

Dorinda understood. Some of the ranchers and farmers weren't keen on their children attending school. A few went so far as to keep them at home. Sheriff Evans appreciated the teachers letting him know about children who stopped showing up. He'd ride out and have a discussion with the parents. Usually, it was the father who insisted he needed his son or daughter at home to keep up with the chores.

She gave the boy an understanding nod. "I'll walk over to the newspaper office during lunch. Perhaps the owners will be able to see us during the last hour of school." She saw the relief on the boy's face.

"All right, everyone back to their studies."

The rest of the day went as most others, with students moving between studies, asking questions, and writing on their slate boards. The walk to the newspaper during lunch proved fruitful. The Kellys were more than willing to meet a little earlier.

When the group made their way along the boardwalk, Dorinda could hear the whispers of the students behind her. Some sounded nervous, others excited. She felt a combination of both.

Approaching the newspaper office, Dorinda paused, turning to the students. "Remember to express your ideas in a clear voice. Share your enthusiasm while being respectful."

Some answered with "Yes, ma'am," while others nodded. Dorinda gave them an encouraging smile, took a deep breath herself, and led them inside.

A bell jangled above the door as they entered the newspaper's front office. A lanky man with spectacles looked up from a rolltop desk. A smile spread across his face as he stood.

"Good morning. You must be the students Mrs. Heaton mentioned. I'm Charley Kelly, and this is my wife, Mrs. Maude Kelly." He gestured to a petite woman, her hair in a tight bun, who stood near a printing press.

The silence extended a moment before one of the girls spoke up. "We're very pleased you agreed to talk with us, Mr. Kelly." The other students smiled, nodding their agreement.

"My eager, young students have an idea they'd like to share with you."

"We're happy to listen," Charley said.

Maude Kelly and Charley pulled up chairs and looked at the students, their expressions open and expectant.

A female student cleared her throat, describing their idea for students to write articles about local events and happenings of interest to the town. One of the male students chimed in about how it would allow them to practice their writing skills.

Another student explained the group's vision for covering a wide range of topics, from school activities to town gossip. The students' enthusiasm was contagious as they took turns speaking.

The Kellys listened intently, asking questions as they learned more about the request.

When the students were finished, Charley leaned toward his wife, whispering near her ear. She whispered back, turning back to the students with a smile. Both stood, Charley providing their decision.

"All right, you've convinced us. We'd be happy to devote a section of the Herald to well-written student submissions. Let's start with one article a week and see how it goes."

The students didn't try to hide their excitement, thanking the Kellys and promising the couple they wouldn't be sorry about giving them a chance. Dorinda let out a relieved breath, overjoyed at their success.

As they made their way back to school, Dorinda congratulated them on their polished presentation. She knew their victory today was the beginning of an exciting new chapter for each of her students.

"Well done, everyone." Dorinda beamed as they entered the almost empty schoolhouse.

Amelia rushed toward Dorinda, Joel right behind

her. "Did it go well?"

"Better than we could've hoped."

"They're going to print our articles once a week, Miss Amelia," one girl beamed.

A male student puffed out his chest. "Think of all the people who'll get to read our articles."

Dorinda smiled as she listened to their ambitious plans for potential story ideas. Their success today had filled them with newfound confidence and purpose.

After everyone left the schoolhouse, Dorinda sat down, relieved and pleased with how the students had conducted themselves.

Her smile faded as her thoughts turned to Dutch. She still hadn't seen him, and it had been several days. Usually, he'd stop by the schoolhouse to check in, tipping his hat to Dorinda as he passed by on his rounds. He hadn't stopped by once this week.

With a sense of unease, Dorinda wondered if he was avoiding her on purpose. Then she recalled what Amelia had told her about Dutch receiving a telegram from Charleston.

Whatever had kept him away, Dorinda had to find a way to help her friend. Dutch shouldn't have to carry any burden alone.

Chapter Eight

Dorinda sat up in bed, her gaze moving around the room before her shoulders slumped. It was still dark, maybe an hour or more before dawn. Dutch's absence gnawed at her, making sleep almost impossible. She had to find him.

Rising, she slipped into her dressing gown and plodded to the kitchen. Coffee sounded good, along with a slice of the cinnamon apple cake she'd made earlier in the week. It was one of Dutch's favorites.

She poured coffee into a cup, taking a quick sip before picking up the plate with cake and setting the items on the table. Dorinda took a seat with a good view out the living room window once the sun rose. Right now, the darkness was black as ink.

Taking a bite of cake, she chewed slowly before swallowing it down with coffee. Her mind moved again to Dutch. She knew something had to be wrong, or he would've stopped by the schoolhouse. He never went more than two days without coming to the school or her house to see Joel.

She was almost certain he'd either ridden to the territorial capital of Big Pine or the Pelletier ranch. Dutch and Luke were old friends, though they didn't see each other often. Still, whenever Dutch had anything difficult to decide, he'd search out Luke.

Placing another bite of cake in her mouth, Dorinda knew where she and Joel would be headed after breakfast. Joel's favorite place was where his uncle lived, and where he could run until he ran out of breath.

She set the plate and empty cup into the sink before returning to the bedroom. Joel still slept, which gave her time to wash up and dress. Hating to wake him, knowing she had to, Dorinda moved to the bed.

"Come on, sweetheart. We're going to ride out to see Uncle Spencer." She shook him with a gentle touch until his eyes opened. "You need to get up so we can go see the ranch."

He looked at her before sitting up. "To see Uncle Spencer?"

"That's right. Now get dressed while I fix breakfast."

Jumping out of bed, he rushed around the bedroom, pulling on his clothes faster than Dorinda could put his breakfast on the table.

Joel tugged at her skirt as they headed the short distance to the jail. "Where are we going?"

"I want to stop at the jail before we go to the ranch."

Dorinda and Joel stepped inside the cool, stone building to see two deputies drinking coffee. "Morning, Mack, Caleb. Have either of you seen Dutch this morning?"

The men exchanged glances before Caleb answered. "Not since yesterday morning. Is everything all right?"

"I'm not sure. He hasn't stopped by the school all week, which is unusual." Dorinda set her hand on Joel's shoulder.

Caleb leaned back in his chair. "Last we saw him was when that telegram arrived. Sent him into a mood, brooding and silent."

Mack nodded in agreement. "He wouldn't say what it was about, just stuffed the telegram in his pocket and stalked off. He hasn't been himself since."

Dorinda absorbed this news. The telegram from Charleston. It had to be about his family. Her heart ached for him. If only she could find him, offer comfort or a listening ear. Anything he needed. She had to keep searching.

"Thank you," she said. "If you see him, please tell him I'm looking for him."

Back outside, Dorinda looked up and down the street. "Let's go to the livery. With luck, Mr. Brandt will have a wagon we can use."

Her legs felt like lead weights as they trudged down the street. Noah hadn't seen Dutch since the day before when he rode out.

"I'd like to rent a wagon. I have an idea where he might be. Plus, it's been a couple weeks since I've seen my brother."

Noah set his hands on his hips and studied her. "Do you plan to go alone?"

"I'm going to the Pelletier ranch. It's not too far, and the weather is fine." She glanced up at the clear blue sky dotted with a few white clouds.

"I know you've driven a wagon before," Noah said. "I'm not comfortable with you riding out to the Pelletier place by yourself."

"I'm going to ride with her, Mr. Brandt." Joel grinned up at Noah.

He smiled down at the boy. "And you'll be a big help." He looked at Dorinda. "The wagon I have is in good shape. I don't rent it out unless it's safe. But what if you break an axel or riders approach?"

"I'll take my scattergun with me." She crossed her arms, glaring at him.

As she stood there, both contemplating their next move, the livery gate swung open. Her pulse quickened, hoping to see Dutch. Instead, a tall, broad-shouldered man with thick black hair and piercing black eyes approached them. He looked to be in his mid-thirties, dressed in an expensive coat, shirt, and pants. On his feet were a pair of elaborately designed black boots. She'd never seen him before, figuring he must be new to Splendor.

The man tipped his hat to Dorinda, stopping a yard away from her and Noah. "Pardon me, ma'am." He looked at Noah. "My name's Nathaniel Burke. I'd like to use one of your horses. For a fee, of course."

Noah indicated a row of stalls. "Those are the horses you can choose from. Where are you headed?"

"I'll be riding to the Pelletier ranch."

A slow grin appeared on Noah's face. "Well, now, that'll work real well."

Burke's brows drew together.

"Mrs. Heaton is renting a wagon to ride out to see her brother, who works for the Pelletiers. Perhaps you could ride along with her."

"It would be my pleasure to accompany her." Burke looked at Dorinda. "If that is acceptable to you, Mrs. Heaton."

She glanced at Noah before looking back at the newcomer. "Yes, that's acceptable. Thank you, Mr. Burke."

Nathaniel Burke rode behind the wagon as Dorinda left town for the Pelletier ranch. She could feel the stranger's eyes boring into her back as they passed the schoolhouse on the ride north. Glancing back, she caught him watching her.

After a while, the trail widened, allowing him to ride beside her. "Did I understand Mr. Brandt to say you have a brother who works for the Pelletiers?"

"Yes."

"Has he been there long?"

"Close to four years." She glanced over at him, a

shiver passing through her. Something about the intensity of his gaze unsettled her. She slapped the lines, quickening their pace, eager to get to the ranch.

Who was this Nathaniel Burke, and what business did he have with the most successful ranchers in western Montana?

"Are you new to Splendor, Mr. Burke?"

He kept his gaze on the trail ahead as if he expected trouble. "Quite new. I purchased a little more than a thousand acres south of Splendor a few months ago. I decided to wait until winter ended before traveling west to see it."

"You mean you bought property without inspecting it?"

"I'm sure it sounds odd. The truth is, I've known Gabe Evans for years. We served together in the Union Army. Gabe heard about the property being for sale, took a ride out to see it, and sent me a letter."

"I see. You trusted his judgment?"

He chuckled. "We saved each other's lives during the war. There are few men I trust more than Gabe."

"Did your family come out with you?"

When he didn't respond, she glanced at him, seeing the amiable features had turned hard. "No. My wife died several years ago of consumption."

"I'm sorry." Her heart ached at the news.

"Thank you. Near the end, it was a blessing. I don't know if you've seen how consumption can ravage a body, but it isn't a disease I'd wish on anyone."

"So I've heard."

"And you, Mrs. Heaton. Was your husband not able to make the trip today?"

Sucking in a breath, she released it on a sigh. "I'm no longer married."

"I'm sorry to hear it."

"He's still alive, Mr. Burke. I sought a divorce."

Nathaniel didn't respond at first. Few people did. Divorces were rare, making her situation awkward.

"Does he still live in Splendor?"

"No. He still works the farm near Salt Lake City."

"I understand the area is inhabited by Mormons. Is that correct?"

"Yes, it is."

Nodding, he didn't reply, continuing to watch the trail ahead. "Mrs. Heaton, there is a group of riders coming toward us. Keep going, and don't stop. I'll find out who they are and their business." Burke moved his coat behind the six-shooter at his waist.

"Mama?" Joel scooted closer to her.

"It will be fine. Mr. Burke is going to talk to them."

When the riders came into view, Dorinda narrowed her gaze, attempting to determine if she'd ever seen them before. Not one looked familiar. The group reined up as the wagon approached. They spread across the trail, making it impossible for her to move through them.

"Gentlemen. If you'd move aside, we'll be on our way." He counted five men. More than he could handle if they drew on him.

"Where you headed?" The man in front rode a few

feet forward.

Joel tucked even closer to his mother when he spied the man. The grizzled features, unkempt black beard and mustache, and menacing grin did nothing to relieve the boy's unease.

"Redemption's Edge. It's up ahead."

"Pretty big spread from what we could see."

"Did you talk to anyone?" Burke asked.

"We did. Asked if they needed help. One of their foremen told us they had more men than they needed and for us to move on. That's what we're doing. Is there a town up ahead?"

"There is. It's a quiet town filled with good people. Keep it in mind when you ride in," Nathaniel said.

The leader of the group eyed him, his hand moving enough to make Burke notice. The man's gaze moved to the wagon carrying a woman and a small boy. His hand shifted back to his saddlehorn.

"Good advice, Mister. Thanks."

Burke touched the brim of his hat. "Anytime."

He turned, waving Dorinda to drive on through. The men moved their horses to the side of the trail, letting her pass. When the wagon had cleared the men, she let out a shaky breath.

"Were they bad men, Mama?"

"I don't know, Joel. Best to be safe, right?"

"I guess so."

Nathaniel didn't catch up to them for several minutes, waiting until the men were out of sight. He knew it didn't mean they wouldn't turn around and ride back. Continuing to check over his shoulder, he rode near the back of the wagon for a bit before coming up alongside it.

"Did you know them, Mr. Burke?"

"I've never seen them before. I just didn't like what I saw."

A slow smile tipped the corners of her mouth. "Joel and I didn't much like the looks of them, either."

Burke chuckled as he watched the trail. A tense half mile passed before he spotted the entrance to the ranch. Riding up the long drive, he noted the number of men watching two men in a corral. They were attempting to tame a horse not too interested in their endeavor.

A couple men walked out of the barn, heading toward the house. One stopped at the sight of the wagon and stared, then began to walk their way.

Dorinda spotted the tall man coming toward them, the sun glistening off his dark red hair. She waved her hand in greeting. Dutch lifted a hand as he continued toward the wagon.

"Good morning, Dorinda."

Joel stood, walked to the side of the wagon, and jumped into Dutch's arms.

"Hey, there," he exclaimed, tightening his arms around Joel.

"We came here to see Uncle Spencer. And to find you. We were looking all over town for you, Dutch."

He looked at Dorinda. "Maybe I should've told you I'd be gone a few days."

She shook her head. "No reason except we were

worried about you, right, Joel?"

"Real worried." He nodded at Dutch, who chuckled, letting the boy slide to the ground.

Burke watched the exchange with interest, trying to decide what the relationship was between Dorinda and Dutch.

She motioned toward the stranger. "Dutch, this is Nathaniel Burke. Mr. Burke, this is Deputy Dutch McFarlin." The two nodded at each other. "He's friends with Sheriff Evans."

"That a fact, Burke?"

"It is. We fought together during the war."

Dutch took the information in, nodding. "He's a good man."

"He is. Gabe encouraged me to ride here to meet the Pelletiers. I bought some acreage south of Splendor. I intend to run cattle."

"There's a lot of good grazing down south. Do you have a piece of Wildflower Creek?"

Burke gave a sharp nod. "I do, plus three springs. I'm negotiating for another five hundred acres that share a property line with me."

"You're going to have yourself a real fine spread," Dutch said, glancing at Dorinda. "Come on up to the house. I'll ask Luke where he has Spencer working today."

He climbed into the wagon, taking the reins from Dorinda as Joel ran up ahead. She glanced over at him, seeing new lines of worry, and signs of sleepless nights.

As soon as they had a private moment, Dorinda

was determined to find out what bothered her friend. What disturbed him, and find out what she could do to help.

Chapter Nine

Nathaniel Burke strode into the expansive ranch house, keen to make a good impression on the Pelletier brothers. Dax and Luke rose from their leather chairs to greet him with firm handshakes.

"Good to meet you, Mr. Burke," Dax said, motioning toward a chair. "Gabe Evans told us you're looking to start up a spread south of town. He also said you were friends during the war."

"That's right. I'm aiming to establish a cattle operation on the thousand acres I purchased." He sat down, looking around the spacious study.

Luke poured three glasses of whiskey. "Well, we can tell you the issues we faced when starting our ranch. It's now the largest spread in the Montana Territory."

As the men discussed land acquisitions and cattle breeding, Nathaniel's gaze drifted to the parlor. Dorinda Heaton's brown hair caught the afternoon light streaming through the windows as she chatted with Rachel and Ginny Pelletier. She met his stare, then looked away.

Nathaniel struggled to focus on the conversation, his mind returning again and again to the enchanting woman. Her shy smile and gentle laugh stirred something within him. The move to Splendor may prove more rewarding than he'd anticipated.

Outside, Dutch led Joel into the large barn, the pungent smells of hay and livestock filling their noses. Joel's eyes widened when he saw Spencer forking hay into the stalls.

"Uncle Spencer!" Joel shouted, running to hug his leg.

Spencer chuckled and ruffled the boy's hair. "Well, hey there, partner. You here to help me with the critters?"

Joel nodded, a broad smile brightening his face. Spencer set down his pitchfork and hoisted the boy up onto his shoulders.

"I've got a surprise for you," he said, carrying Joel over to a stall where a tabby cat nursed a litter of mewing kittens. Joel gasped in delight at the tiny furballs.

Dutch leaned on the stall door, smiling as he watched their interaction.

"He sure does love his Uncle Spencer," Dutch remarked.

"That's 'cause I'm the fun one," Spencer replied with a wink. He set Joel down to pet the kittens.

Spencer then led them over to a pregnant cow. "Ole Bessie here is gonna have herself a calf real soon," he told Joel. The boy pressed his small hands to the cow's swollen belly in fascination.

After a bit, Spencer glanced at Dutch. "Maybe Joel could stay the night. Be good for him to get some time on the ranch."

Dutch nodded. "You'd have to ask Dorinda."

Later in the afternoon, Dorinda drove the wagon back toward town. She'd allowed Joel to spend the night, with Spencer bringing him back to town the next day. To her surprise, Nathaniel Burke rode up alongside her.

"Mrs. Heaton," he greeted her.

"Mr. Burke. I thought you were staying at the Pelletier ranch for supper." Dorinda increased the wagon's pace.

Nathaniel kept up. "Please, call me Nathaniel. I was hoping I might persuade you to join me for supper this evening at McCall's."

Dorinda hesitated. She'd planned on cooking a simple meal back at her house. And yet the charming newcomer intrigued her.

"That's very kind of you."

Nathaniel flashed a grin. "Wonderful, I'll come by this evening to escort you." He tipped his hat and rode ahead of the wagon several yards, leaving Dorinda flustered. She chided herself even as her heart quickened.

When they arrived in town, Nathaniel helped Dorinda down from the wagon. His hand lingered on hers a moment longer than expected.

"Until this evening." Dorinda watched him go, a mix of uncertainty and anticipation swirling within her.

Dorinda stood outside the small schoolhouse, watching the last students leave for the day. For a few minutes, she thought of the lovely evening spent over supper with Nathaniel. He wasn't at all as she'd first thought.

They'd spoken of his plan to run cattle, and her challenges providing schooling as the town's population exploded. The budget was terribly tight, she'd explained to Nathaniel over slices of Betts's incredible custard pie.

She looked back inside the schoolhouse and sighed, thinking of the leaky roof and lack of books and supplies.

"Good afternoon, Mrs. Heaton," said a familiar voice. She turned to see Nathaniel walking toward her. "I thought I'd find you here."

"Mr. Burke," Dorinda replied.

"Please, I've asked you to call me Nathaniel." He smiled. "After our conversation at supper Saturday night, I wanted to see for myself what the school needs. You mentioned how the budget doesn't allow for the increasing number of students. Do you have a moment to let me see inside?"

Dorinda nodded, a bit surprised. "Miss Amelia and I make do with what we have, but yes, the budget is quite small. Please..." She motioned for him to go inside.

She showed him the desks and supplies they used. Then she pulled out the school roster. Counting the number of students, then the number of desks, it was obvious how they were short basic necessities.

Nathaniel stroked his chin thoughtfully. "Well, what if I made a donation? Enough to purchase additional desks, books, slates, and slate pencils."

"Oh, but why would you do such a thing?" Dorinda was taken aback by his generosity.

He shrugged. "I believe in investing in the future. Education is the best investment there is." His eyes twinkled at her. "Consider it my way of contributing to the town I hope will become my home."

Dorinda stared at him, speechless. With Nathaniel's donation, she and Amelia could provide their students with the materials they deserved. She imagined the children's joy at additional desks and supplies.

"That's incredibly generous of you," she said earnestly. "The impact on our students will be tremendous. You have my deepest gratitude."

"It's my pleasure. I'd like to invite you and Joel to supper at the boardinghouse tonight. What do you say?"

"I'm certain both of us would love to join you."

"I'll stop by your house about five and escort you."

As he strode away, Dorinda blinked back grateful tears. She'd misjudged the newcomer. Beneath his roguish exterior lay a good heart. Yet she still felt a twinge of hesitation about him. Only time would tell if he was truly as selfless as he appeared. For now, she allowed herself to feel a glimmer of hope.

Dutch stood outside the mercantile late that afternoon, talking with Morgan as he watched Dorinda, Joel, and Nathaniel walk along the boardwalk. Though he kept his expression impassive, inside, he was churning.

It bothered him to see Dorinda looking so relaxed and happy with the newcomer. Laughing at something Nathaniel said, her eyes bright with interest. Dutch's jaw tightened.

He and Dorinda had been friends for ages, though he'd always felt an unspoken connection, hinting at something more. The timing had never been right. There had always been reasons to remain good friends, and nothing more.

But now, seeing Nathaniel wooing Dorinda with such ease, Dutch was seized by an almost panicked sense of regret. What if he'd waited too long? The thought was like a punch to the gut.

As Nathaniel opened the boardinghouse restaurant door for Dorinda and Joel, Dutch balled a hand into a fist. He had to talk to her, tell her how he really felt. He wanted to make it clear she had another option besides the charming rancher.

His heart pounding, Dutch started toward the boardinghouse. Just as he reached the door, Morgan grabbed his arm.

"You don't want to do this tonight, Dutch."

Dutch glared at him, then released a hot breath, nodding. "You're right."

"You need time to think this through. A month ago, you told me you and Dorinda would never be more than good friends. If you've changed your mind, you should talk to her in private. Not in a crowded restaurant."

The door opened as a couple left. He could hear Dorinda laugh. The sound, usually so pleasing, now grated on Dutch.

Nodding, he turned around and headed across the street toward the jail. Morgan was right. Before he spoke with Dorinda, he needed to figure out if he wanted more than friendship from her or for their relationship to remain good friends.

Chapter Ten

Dorinda busied herself setting the table, the clinking of plates and utensils a comforting rhythm as she prepared supper. Though their little home was modest, she took pride in keeping it homey and welcoming. The enticing aroma of roast beef filled the house, and Dorinda's stomach rumbled in anticipation.

"Smells good, Mama." Joel rushed into the kitchen from the bedroom, having washed up for supper.

She smiled at her boy. "Well, come on and sit down. It's just about ready."

Joel hurried to do as told, almost knocking over his chair in his haste. Dorinda chuckled and shook her head. Her sweet boy, always hungry as a bear in springtime.

She spooned the roast, potatoes, and vegetables onto plates when an unexpected knock at the door made her jump. Frowning, Dorinda set down the large spoon and went to see who could be calling at this hour. She opened the door, and her breath caught in her throat.

Jared.

Her ex-husband's face was weary but determined, his hat in hand. Dorinda stared, stunned to silence. A tide of emotions rose up in her—anger, hurt, longing. She hadn't seen Jared since he'd followed her to Splendor when she and Joel fled the farm.

Dorinda found her voice. "What are you doing here?" The words came out sharp as broken glass.

Jared winced but held her gaze. "Dorinda, I...I had to see you. To try and make things right." He hesitated. "May I come in?"

She wavered, gripping the doorframe until her knuckles turned white. The past clawed at her, threatening to drag her back. The present beckoned, too, offering the second chance she'd hoped for.

Stepping back, she allowed Jared to enter. He removed his hat. They stood in awkward silence as Dorinda closed the door behind him.

"Papa!" Joel rushed to his father, who took him into his arms and stood.

"You are so big."

"I know. I'm almost as big as you."

Jared looked away as his eyes filled. "Yes, almost."

"I missed you, Papa."

Dorinda wrapped her arms around herself, as if to shield against the onslaught of emotions.

"I've missed you, too, son. And I've missed you, Dorinda."

Jared set Joel on the floor, though his son stayed next to him.

She nodded, swallowing the knot of emotion lodged in her throat. "I know I shouldn't, but I've missed you, too, Jared," she admitted.

He nodded, his eyes downcast. "I understand. What I did...it was unforgivable." He looked up at her, his face etched with shame and regret. "I don't expect you to forgive me. But I had to try. Had to tell you how sorry I am, how much I regret everything."

Dorinda searched his face, looking for any sign of deception. All she saw was humility. Could it be true? Could the man who'd hurt her so deeply be repentant?

"Please," Jared implored. "All I ask is for you to consider..." He glanced at Joel and shook his head. "Perhaps we could speak later."

Before Dorinda could respond, Joel spoke up. "Mama, I'm starvin'! Papa, can you eat with us?"

Jared's face softened. "Perhaps, son," he said in a gentle voice. "It depends on your mother."

"Please, Mama, can Papa stay for supper?"

Dorinda hesitated a moment before nodding. "Yes. We have plenty, Jared."

"Now you have to stay, Papa."

She glanced away, feeling pulled in too many directions. Releasing a heavy breath, she walked back to the kitchen, taking down another plate.

Watching as Jared interacted with Joel, she served up the remaining roast. She had to look away, her heart a jumble of emotions.

Seeing Jared play and joke with their son again brought back fond memories of the happy days of their marriage. But she couldn't forget the pain and betrayal when he'd brought a second wife into their home. He'd promised never to ruin their love by taking a second wife. Instead, he'd buckled to pressure from the elders.

Dorinda's love and desire for Jared had died a little every day afterward until she finally packed her bags and left with Joel.

"Supper's ready," she called, and winced. They were the same words she used to call out when they were a family.

She saw the earnestness in Jared's eyes as he tried to connect with her over supper. He seemed so repentant for all he'd put them through. But how could she ever trust him again after he'd broken a promise which meant everything to her?

After Jared had put Joel to bed, he returned to the living room and sat down at the opposite end of the sofa from where Dorinda worked on a needlepoint.

"What are you working on?"

"It's an image of a horse with a boy standing alongside."

"Joel?"

She glanced up. "Yes. A friend took us riding a while ago. Joel loved it. He's always asking to go again."

"A friend?"

Setting the needlepoint in her lap, she nodded. "Yes. He's a deputy who's taken an interest in Joel. We've become friends." She left it at that, uninterested in saying more about her complicated friendship with Dutch.

"I know I don't deserve your trust. But I swear on my life I will never hurt you or Joel again. Losing you both because of my broken promise was the biggest mistake I ever made."

He moved closer, his eyes pleading. "Come back to the farm, Dorinda. It's not the same without you. I need you. Joel needs his mama and papa together."

Dorinda felt paralyzed. Part of her wanted to believe Jared had changed, but the scars ran so deep.

"It's not that simple," she whispered. "What about Clara?"

"She left. Clara wasn't cut out for chores around the farm."

"I'm sorry your marriage with her wasn't what you'd hoped."

"It's best she's gone, Dorinda. I never loved her. I'm not certain I liked her."

She glanced away, not quite able to hide the smile his words brought.

Jared clasped her hands in his. "Tell me what I need to do to make this right. I'll do whatever it takes to get you and Joel back."

Dorinda searched Jared's face. For the first time, she saw true anguish in the creases of his brow. This was not the same man she'd left after a broken promise ruined their love. Something had shifted in him. Was it enough?

"I need time." She pulled her hands away. "I can't make such a decision without a great deal of thought."

Jared looked pained but nodded. "I understand. Take all the time you need. I'll wait for you, Dorinda.

No matter how long it takes."

She let out a shaky breath as Jared took his leave. The decision before her felt like an impossible weight. She knew deep down that for better or worse, this moment would define the rest of her life.

Dorinda sank into a chair in the bedroom, emotionally spent. In the bed, Joel sat up, rubbing his sleepy eyes.

"Is Pa still here?" he asked.

She composed herself and nodded. "Yes. He had no place to stay, so he's going to bed down on the sofa."

He perked up. "Is he gonna stay with us now?"

Her heart constricted. "We aren't sure yet. We're still talking about it."

"I miss Papa."

"I know you do. Now, it's time for you to go back to sleep." She tucked the covers around him. As he drifted off, she pressed a soft kiss to his forehead. Her heart ached at the innocent longing in her son's face. He deserved to have his father in his life. But at what cost?

With Joel asleep, she changed into her sleeping gown, washed her face, and brushed her hair. She wondered if Jared had been able to get to sleep. The sofa didn't accommodate his long frame, but there was nothing to do about it.

The clock on her dresser ticked in the silence. Doubts and fears swirled in her mind. What was she to do?

Stretching out under the covers, she stared into the darkness. The conversation with Jared rolled inside her mind. He'd been sincere in his regret, she was certain of it.

The next day, as Dorinda and Amelia tidied up after the last students had left, they heard boots on the wood floor and looked up. Dutch stood near the door with his hat in his hands.

"Afternoon, ladies," he said.

"Deputy McFarlin," Amelia said, glancing at Dorinda. "Well, I need to start for home. See you in the morning."

Once she'd left, Dutch walked forward, stopping a few feet from Dorinda. "I saw a man talking with Joel, and introduced myself."

"My ex-husband, Jared. He traveled here to ask me to return to the farm."

He set his hat on the desk, leaning against the edge. "I'm sure this is difficult for you. How are you holding up?"

She gave him a tired smile. "As well as can be expected. I'm glad you're back in town." She sighed, lowering herself into a chair.

"I don't know what I'm going to do. He seems so

sincere in his regret about taking a second wife." Looking at Dutch, she allowed a slight smile to appear. "Clara left him. Chores were too much for her. I'm not surprised. She never lifted a hand to help while Joel and I still lived at the farm."

"For what it's worth, seems to me like you're handling his appearance well."

Dorinda laughed. "Trust me. I'm not as calm as I might appear."

Silence enveloped them for several minutes before Dutch spoke. "Have you decided what you'll do?"

She shook her head. "I'm torn. Half of me wants to return to the farm, if only for Joel's sake. But the other half…"

"You're afraid," he finished.

Dorinda nodded, tears glistening in her eyes. "What if I go back and he hurts me again? Breaks my trust all over? I just don't know if I can ever trust him again."

He leaned toward her, his expression earnest. "Now you listen here. Whatever you decide, I'll support you one hundred percent. This is your home now. But if you decide to return to Jared and he reverts to his old ways, I'll travel to Salt Lake City and haul you and Joel back to Splendor."

Despite herself, she laughed. She placed a hand on Dutch's arm. "Thank you. I can't tell you how much that means."

He placed his hand over hers. "Anytime."

Dorinda felt the weight on her shoulders lighten, if only a little.

Chapter Eleven

Dorinda's heart felt heavy as she walked home from school alone that afternoon. After renting a horse from Noah, Jared had taken Joel for a ride on a trail north of town. When they returned, they would have supper at the house, opening what she knew would be another round of talks.

She thought of Dutch's visit to the school. Though Dutch's support meant the world to her, she was no closer to deciding whether to give Jared another chance or stay in Splendor.

Her brief stop at the meat market extended when Nathaniel Burke walked inside. He was the last person she wanted to run into.

"Dorinda. How are you?"

"I'm fine, Nathaniel. And you?"

"Very good. I've met with a man from the Pelletier ranch who's able to draw plans for a house, barn, and other buildings on my property. Work will begin soon."

"How wonderful. Who is it?"

"Bull Mason. Do you know him?"

"I do. I'm sure he'll do an excellent job for you. What brings you into the market today?"

"Just getting to know the town. I learned to cook after my wife passed. A man at the St. James hotel recommended this store." Nathaniel looked around. "It's more than a meat market."

"Oh, yes. Mrs. Caulfield bakes all the breads, including the sweet breads, rolls, and pastries. Though, in my opinion, May Covington at the Eagle's Nest, is the best pastry chef in Splendor. Unfortunately, she has little time to bake for those not eating at the restaurant."

"Mrs. Heaton, what can I get for you today?" Mr. Caulfield looked at her from over his display counter.

"Excuse me, Nathaniel. I need to make my purchases and be on my way." She gave her order and turned back to him.

"Do you have an evening free for supper?" he asked.

She hesitated a moment. "I'm not sure. An unexpected visitor is in town. He..."

A brow rose. "He?"

She sighed, her heart sinking. "My ex-husband. He, well..."

"Wants you back."

Her eyes widened. "How did you know?"

"It's not hard, Dorinda. If it were me, I'd want you back."

As she approached the little house she rented from Noah, Dorinda thought of Nathaniel's comment about the reason Jared had traveled to Splendor. She hadn't shared her reason for seeking a divorce with Nathaniel, so he had no idea why she'd left her husband. Perhaps the newcomer was a particularly perceptive man.

Entering her home, she stoked the fire and set to work preparing chicken fricassee. While working, she considered the different men in her life, and the decision she'd need to make soon.

There was no doubt Jared still held a place in her heart. They'd been so happy once. The chores never bothered her, and when Joel was born, she'd taken on the additional responsibilities with joy. She'd never imagined Jared would break his promise and bring a second wife into their home. Her heart still ached whenever she recalled Clara entering their small home for the first time. The marriage with Jared had died that day.

Her mind shifted to Nathaniel. She enjoyed his company and believed they might be able to build a future together. His plans for a ranch suited her and would provide Joel with an opportunity to own a horse and learn ranching. Then again, he could do the same by spending time with Spencer at the Pelletier ranch. Did she think she could love Nathaniel? She had no answer.

Then there was Dutch. They'd become great friends over the time she'd lived in Splendor, and he cared about, maybe loved, Joel. She'd often wondered if they could build a future together. First, Dutch would have to show an interest in her beyond friendship. Could she marry Dutch? Her heart beat faster at the thought. It always did whenever the handsome, broad-shouldered deputy was near. Did her heart speed up when Jared arrived the night before? She didn't recall.

The front door burst open, and Joel rushed inside, followed by Jared. "Mama!" Joel cried, barreling into her skirts.

Dorinda stroked his hair. "There's my sweet boy. Did you have a good ride?"

"Uh-huh! We rode past a pond and saw cows and horses and lots of birds."

"You'll have to come with us next time." Jared stood near the dining table, watching.

"I'd love to," Dorinda answered, though it wasn't an image of Jared on a horse beside her. Instead, Dutch rode his tall, bay gelding. She shook her head, returning her attention to the meal she was preparing.

"Why don't you do your reading while I finish with supper, Joel," she suggested.

Shoulders slumping, he moved away from her. "All right." Passing his father, he walked into the bedroom and closed the door.

"Joel rides well," Jared said, joining her in the kitchen. "He told me the two of you and a man named Dutch rode to a lagoon not long ago."

"The deputy I told you about. Dutch McFarlin. He's good with Joel."

"Ah…" Jared leaned against the counter, watching her work.

"He stops by the school a couple days each week to visit. I think he's lonely."

"I see." He pulled out a chair at the table and sat down. "Joel mentioned someone taking him from school."

She whirled toward Jared. "What? Are you saying he told you about going missing?"

Jared sat up straighter. "Missing? No, he didn't say that. He said a woman came to the school and needed help. Joel went with her. That's all he told me."

Taking a chair next to him, she wrapped her arms around her middle. "He went missing for two days, Jared. Joel disappeared from the schoolyard. No one saw him leave. The entire town searched for him."

"And you found him?"

"No. He showed up back at the schoolyard, a little dazed but unhurt. He wouldn't talk for days. Did he give you the woman's name?"

"No. I've told you all he shared with me."

"But he said it was a woman?"

"Yes."

"After supper, I must go to the jail and let Gabe know what he told you."

"Gabe?"

"He's the sheriff. If he's not there, I'll have to go to

his home." She shook her head. "I don't believe anyone considered a woman taking Joel."

The bedroom door opened, and a smiling Joel emerged with a paper in his hand. He presented Dorinda with a crude but precious drawing depicting the three of them. His mother, father, and Joel were standing together on a farm, holding hands and smiling.

"It's our family, back home on the farm," Joel explained.

Her throat tightened with emotion. She pulled Joel close. "What a wonderful drawing."

"Papa said if we go back to the farm, we can be a family again."

She shot a pained look at Jared. She'd wanted to shield Joel from the complicated truth, but Jared's presence had muddied the waters.

"It's not that simple, sweetheart. Papa and I..." Dorinda paused, cautious about what to say. "We have a lot we need to work through."

"Don't you want us to be a family?" Joel's eyes grew wide.

"Joel," Jared said. "The drawing is wonderful. Now please put the drawing away and continue your reading."

Excitement fading, Joel looked between his parents before returning to the bedroom.

Dorinda rose with the sun the next morning, having tossed and turned all night. She knew the idea of a reunited family now danced in Joel's head, as dangerous as it was alluring.

The only certainty she faced was the ache of indecision, and the knowledge that whatever she decided, someone she loved would be hurt.

Dorinda moved through the small home, not wanting to disturb Jared or Joel. Coffee brewed on the stove, indicating Jared was already up.

She found him sitting on the front porch step, gazing out at the dawn light spreading across the tops of the horizon. He turned at the sound of the door opening behind him.

"Morning," he said.

"Morning." She leaned against the porch railing, staring sightlessly into the distance as she gathered her turbulent thoughts.

"Jared, I...I just don't know. My life is here now, I have a job, friends..." Her voice trailed off helplessly.

Jared's face was etched with pain. "You also still have me, Dorinda. And Joel has a father. I know I failed you before, but I aim to spend the rest of my days making it up to you and Joel." His voice dropped. "If you'll let me."

Dorinda bit her lip. Could she risk abandoning her new life on his words? Before she could reply, the sound of an approaching rider drew their attention.

It was Dutch, his familiar face creasing into a smile as he reined up in front of her house. Dorinda exhaled in relief at the sight of him.

"Good morning," Dutch called out as he dismounted. His gaze moved from Dorinda to Jared, no trace of surprise flickering across his features.

"Jared." He held out his hand. "Dutch McLarin. We met earlier. I'm a friend of Dorinda's..."

Dutch shook Jared's hand firmly, his keen eyes assessing the situation. He could sense Dorinda's inner conflict as clearly as if it were written across her forehead.

"Pleasure to meet you." Jared's tone was polite, if wary. His jaw tightened as he assessed the newcomer.

"Likewise," Dutch said. "I stopped by to see if Joel would like to go fishing with me on Saturday."

Dorinda collected herself, touched by his thoughtfulness. "I'm certain he would. It will depend on how long Jared is in town." She looked at her ex-husband, noting the sadness in his eyes.

"How about I stop by Friday after school so you can let me know?"

"That would be fine, Dutch."

"Well, I should be going. But stop by anytime if you need anything." He walked back to his bay gelding and swung into the saddle.

"Thank you," she called after him, hoping he understood her deeper gratitude. Dutch tipped his hat and rode off.

She took a deep breath before turning back to Jared. His dark eyes were fixed on her, his anguish plain. Her heart constricted. Despite everything, she'd never stopped caring for him. But the past could not be undone. She sat down beside him.

"I'm sorry, Jared. It's too soon to give you an answer."

Jared's shoulders slumped, but he nodded. "I understand. Take all the time you need." He hesitated. "I'll be staying at the small boardinghouse across from the church for a few days."

Dorinda managed a weak smile. "I'll let you know what I decide." It was the best she could offer him for now.

Jared donned his hat, his eyes lingering on her face as if to memorize it. Then he turned and made his way to where his horse was hitched. With a final glance back at Dorinda, he mounted up and rode away down the trail, a lone figure fading into the distance.

Dorinda stood there for a long moment after Jared disappeared from view, her mind and emotions swirling. She'd never expected to see him again after his brief trip to Montana, not long after she and Joel arrived. His sudden reappearance now had shaken the fragile life she'd built in Splendor.

A gentle hand on her arm made her jump. She turned to see Joel looking up at her, still wearing pajamas, his young face etched with concern.

"Are you okay, Mama?"

She composed herself, not wanting to worry her son. "I'm fine."

Joel glanced down the road where Jared had ridden off. "Is Papa gone?"

Dorinda swallowed hard. "Yes. He has taken a room at the boardinghouse near the church. He'll still be in town for a few days."

"When he leaves, can we go with him?"

His innocent enthusiasm stabbed at Dorinda's heart.

"I don't know yet, sweetheart," she said gently. "It's a big decision."

Joel looked disappointed but didn't argue.

Dorinda stroked his hair. "Why don't you go on inside and wash up? I'll get breakfast ready, then we need to leave for school."

Joel hurried into the house. Dorinda followed at a slow pace, her thoughts swirling like the dust whirl-winds that whipped across the prairie.

Chapter Twelve

Nathaniel Burke and Bull Mason walked along the ridge overlooking Wildfire Creek, and the thousand sprawling acres on both sides. Nathaniel owned every inch, with plans to buy more land as soon as the opportunity arose.

"There's a fine spot for the ranch house," Bull said, gesturing to a flat area near a copse of lodgepole pines. "Good drainage, plenty of room for outbuildings, and a view of the creek valley."

Nathaniel nodded. "I believe you're right. The barn and bunkhouse could be placed to the west of the house." He pointed toward a grassy meadow downstream. "And put the well somewhere between."

"My thoughts exactly," Bull said. "It'll be a good spot for the cattle in winter."

"Agreed." Nathaniel kicked a stone over the edge, watching it tumble down the steep bank toward the creek.

Nathaniel gazed out at the peaks framing the valley. "I can see this land supporting a prosperous ranch. It will take work, something I'm used to."

Bull made notes in the small journal he'd brought with him. "You're right. It'll take some doing, but you'll build yourself one fine spread here."

Nathaniel clasped Bull's shoulder, a grin breaking through his chiseled face. "That I will, my friend. That I will."

With a last look over Nathaniel's future home, they turned and headed back to their horses. Both were keen to draw up plans for the ranch that would make Nathaniel's dreams a reality.

Nathaniel and Bull made their way back into town, tired from surveying the land but invigorated by the opportunity ahead. As they reached Splendor's main street, Nathaniel nodded toward the boardinghouse.

"Let's stop in for some lunch. I'm famished after all the walking."

Bull agreed, as eager for a hot meal as Nathaniel. Inside, they found a table by the window and ordered steaming bowls of venison stew. They continued discussing plans for the ranch over their meals, debating the best places to situate the house, barn, and bunkhouse.

Their conversation was interrupted when the front door swung open, and Luke Pelletier strode in, followed by his friend, Dutch McFarlin. Spotting Nathaniel and Bull, Luke gave a friendly wave and walked over.

"Nathaniel, Bull," he greeted them. "Mind if we join you?"

"Not at all." Nathaniel motioned to the empty chairs at their table. "What brings you into town today?" he asked after they placed their orders.

Before Luke could respond, a sudden commotion erupted outside. Shouts and startled cries echoed up and down the street as the urgent pounding of hooves approached. The men exchanged puzzled glances, then rushed to the windows to see what was happening.

To their shock, they saw a massive herd of cattle stampeding down the main road, driven into a frenzy. People scrambled to get out of the way as the rampaging animals crashed into wagons, knocked over railings, and barreled through the streets, leaving chaos and destruction in their wake. Gunshots rang out as some tried unsuccessfully to turn the stampede, but the maddened cattle were beyond control.

"Good lord!" Dutch exclaimed over the din. "Where did they come from?"

Luke shook his head, brow furrowed. "I don't know, but someone stirred them up real good. Running through town didn't happen by chance."

The men watched as the stampede trampled everything in its path. Suddenly, one unfortunate soul, who'd been slow to react, was tossed into the air by the cattle's horns and landed hard on the packed dirt road.

"He's not moving, we've got to help him." Bull was already rushing for the door with the others on his heels. They plunged into the chaos, desperate to aid the injured man as the last of the rampaging herd thundered past, leaving wreckage and clouds of dust in their wake.

The once bustling Frontier Street now looked like a disaster zone. Wagons were overturned, storefronts smashed, and merchandise strewn all about. Towns-people emerged from where they had taken shelter, faces stricken as they took in the damage.

Nathaniel, Dutch, Luke, and Bull hurried over to where the man lay unmoving in the dirt. As they got closer, they could see his legs were badly broken, bent at unnatural angles. Luke knelt to check his pulse.

"He's alive, but barely. We need to get him to the doctor."

Luke and Dutch lifted the man, groaning in pain even unconscious, while Bull and Nathaniel support-ed his legs. They carried him toward the clinic as carefully as possible.

"Easy now, we've got you," Nathaniel murmured.

The man's eyes fluttered as he moaned again. Dutch recognized him as one of the local ranch hands.

All around them, other people were emerging to survey the aftermath. Men righted overturned wagons while women comforted crying children. The bodies of two horses lay trampled and lifeless near the bank. An older couple stood over them, the man removing his hat in respect.

"It could've been a whole lot worse," Bull com-mented as they moved through the scene. "I hope they catch whoever did this."

The others nodded. It was an act of sheer malice

to drive a herd through town this way. For now, their focus was on getting this poor man to the doctor. Questions of who and why would have to wait.

The men carried the injured ranch hand into the clinic. As they approached, Doctor Clay McCord was already waiting at the door, having heard the commotion.

"Bring him in. Put him in the first room," he urged them.

They laid the man on the examination table. Doc McCord assessed his injuries, his experienced hands probing the man's legs.

"Both legs are broken. Maybe some internal injuries. I'll do what I can for him." He looked up at the men gathered around the table. "Do you know his name?"

The four shook their heads. "He's a ranch hand somewhere around here, but that's all I know about him," Dutch said.

"All right. I've got him. I'd appreciate it if you'd check for anyone else with injuries and bring them here. Doctor Ralston will be here soon to help."

They nodded, knowing the doctor was right. As much as they wanted to make sure the man would live, there were larger questions needing answers.

Stepping outside, they saw Gabe organizing riders to track the cattle herd. Men were saddling up to join him, armed and ready to ride.

"Gabe!" Luke called out as they approached. "We're with you."

The sheriff nodded, unsurprised by their offer of

help. "Good. We'll need some extra guns in case whoever stampeded the herd return."

The four men rushed to the livery and mounted up alongside the rest of the group. Hooves pounded on the road leading south of town.

The men rode hard, following the clear trail left by the stampeding herd. It wasn't long before the cattle came into view, milling about in a grassy valley a few miles from town.

As they got closer, Bull's sharp eyes picked out the brand seared into the animals' hides. It was a crooked H hanging from a sideways V.

"Those are Hank Varley's cattle," Bull said with certainty. The older rancher lived about ten miles northeast of town.

"Doesn't make sense for Varley to stampede his own herd," Dutch muttered.

Gabe nodded in agreement. "You're right. Something strange is going on here."

The thunder of approaching hooves drew their attention. A lone rider came galloping up, reining in as he reached the group.

"It's Varley," Bull said.

"Sheriff, I came as quick as I could. Somebody stole my cattle and stampeded them toward town." He was a tall, wiry man with a thick mustache.

"Tell me what happened."

"Me and a couple ranch hands were moving the herd south when these riders appeared. They tied us up and took the herd. I got loose, freed the others, and we rode to town." He shook his head in disgust.

"I saw the damage, Sheriff..."

Gabe held up a hand. "It's not your fault, Hank. We need to find the men who took the cattle."

As the lawmen spoke with Varley, piecing together the odd events, the sound of more racing hooves approached. A fresh horse lathered with sweat rode up carrying Deputy Caleb Covington.

"Sheriff!" Caleb called out urgently. "The bank's been robbed!"

Sheriff Evans rode back into town, his keen eyes surveying the aftermath of the chaos. Broken glass and splintered wood littered the street. Townsfolk worked to clear debris and repair damaged storefronts.

He spotted two of his deputies, brothers Hex and Zeke Boudreaux, helping to board up the general store's smashed window. Owner, Stan Petermann, gave Gabe a curt nod when he rode past.

Gabe continued on to the bank. Horace Clausen, the bank president, stood outside talking with attorneys Francesca Boudreaux and Griffin MacKenzie. Gabe dismounted and approached.

"Tell me what happened, Horace."

"Four gunmen entered the bank while the cattle were still stampeding. They got what we had out front and the small amount stored in the safe behind my office." Horace wiped his brow with a handkerchief before stuffing it in a pocket. "We were lucky. No one was hurt, and the thieves knew nothing about our hidden safe."

Horace had the foresight years earlier to build a hidden room where a larger safe held the majority of the money on deposit.

"Smart move, using cattle to divert attention from the robbery," Francesca said.

Griffin gave a slow nod. "A brilliant tactic. No tracks or signs left behind, and the townsfolk trying to get out of the cattle's way. I doubt anyone saw which way the outlaws rode out of town. What's your plan, Gabe?"

"Talk to anyone who may have seen the men leave the bank. I'll round up my deputies and get them canvassing the town."

Griffin nodded across the street. "There are three across the street, helping Olivia McCord and Josie Lucero patch up a broken front window and the damaged entry door of the Emporium."

Gabe turned to see Hawke DeBell, Shane Banderas, and Cole Santori engrossed in their work. "They can start canvassing the town after they're finished with the repairs. Let me know if any of you think of anything I should know." He tipped his hat at Francesca before wheeling around to cross the street.

He spoke to Hawke, Shane, and Cole, receiving nods in return. Gabe then said a few words to Olivia and Josie before striding along the boardwalk to locate the rest of his men.

Dutch left the Dixie and looked up and down the street. Spotting Gabe, he met him partway. "I spoke to the new bartender, Jeb, and couple of men inside the Dixie." He lowered his voice. "Word is, two strangers came into town yesterday. No one had seen them before. They sat at the window facing the bank. Jeb said they were glancing around as they spoke, making sure no one heard them."

"Could Jeb or the other two men describe them?" Gabe asked.

"One of them was tall with a spotty black and gray beard. He wore a black, flat-brimmed gambler hat, and there were two six-shooters on his hips. A scar wound down his face from his temple to his chin." Dutch demonstrated by using a finger to draw a ragged line down his face. "The other fella was the opposite. Short, round, with huge brown eyes. He was clean-shaven and wore a dirty, light-colored open crown hat. I could go through the wanted posters and have Jeb look over the best matches."

"Good idea. Go ahead and get started. I'm going to have the other deputies talk to the townsfolk to see if anybody saw something we can use."

Dutch jogged across the street to the jail, stopped a moment, and looked around when he reached the boardwalk. Dorinda stood on the stoop of the schoolhouse, staring straight at him. She lifted her hand in greeting. He responded, then headed into the jail.

Inside, he grabbed the wanted posters from a drawer and sorted through them. It didn't take long to locate two matching Jeb's description of the men. He added a few more before gathering up the posters and returning to the Dixie.

Jeb moved to join Dutch at the end of the bar. The bartender stared down at each poster, taking his time before setting two aside. He tapped a finger on each one.

"These are the men, Dutch."

"No doubt?"

"None. If a judge asks, I'll swear to it."

Gabe chose not to form a posse to pursue the two men Jeb identified. Instead, he sent telegrams to Sheriff Parker Sterling in Big Pine and several other lawmen throughout the Montana Territory, Wyoming, and Idaho. Splendor returned to normal, townsfolk carrying on as if a herd of cattle hadn't swarmed the main street.

Chapter Thirteen

Dorinda and Joel strode along the street, talking as they made their way toward the schoolhouse for another day of lessons. She and Amelia had a surprise planned for the children, and she was anxious to set it up before they arrived.

Without warning, a haggard figure stepped out from an alcove, blocking their path. Joel gasped, grabbing his mother's hand as he took in the woman's ominous presence. Deep creases lined her face. Her stark black eyes were encased in sallow, puffy skin. Strands of brittle gray hair peeked out from under her tattered black hood.

"Excuse us, ma'am." Dorinda attempted to guide Joel around the older woman, but she shifted and continued to impede their progress. She raised a bony hand, extending one crooked finger to point at Joel. "You..." she rasped out, her gaze never wavering from Joel. "You..." she repeated in a more menacing tone, taking a step toward him.

Dorinda's heart hammered in her chest. Gripping

Joel's hand, she steered him off the boardwalk and into the street, hurrying past the stranger whose piercing gaze followed their every move. They rushed through the jailhouse doors, chests heaving, coming to a stop at the sight of Dutch and Hawke DeBell staring at them. Joel dropped his mother's hand, charging toward Dutch to wrap his arms around the deputy's legs.

"Outside...a woman..." Dorinda began, then faltered as she saw the confusion on the men's faces.

Still catching her breath, Dorinda explained the odd encounter as Joel clung to Dutch's legs. She recounted the woman's haunting appearance and unsettling behavior, conveying her confusion and disquiet.

Dutch's expression turned grim. "You two stay put," he instructed. "Hawke and I will find this woman."

"We'll get to the bottom of this, ma'am," Hawke vowed, touching the brim of his hat. The men turned and strode outside, closing the door behind them.

Dorinda watched through the window as Dutch and Hawke disappeared out of view. Despite their reassurances, unease still twisted in her gut. She couldn't shake the image of the woman's piercing stare and crooked finger pointed at her son.

She sank into a chair. Joel stayed close to her, his small hand holding fast to hers. She stroked his hair, wishing she could erase the morning's distress. Her thoughts drifted back to the day Joel disappeared, guilt and anxiety welling up anew.

After some time, the deputies returned, their boots thudding across the wooden floor.

"Any luck finding her?" Dorinda asked.

Hawke shook his head, his expression grim. "No sign of the woman yet. It's as if she vanished into thin air."

"We questioned the shop owners and folks around town," Dutch said. "Some have seen her around, but no one knows anything about her."

Her shoulders slumped. She'd hoped the woman would be found and questioned. Had she overreacted? Was she a harmless old woman posing no threat?

Dutch stepped closer, his voice low. "Until we get this sorted, I don't want you and Joel walking to and from the school alone."

Dorinda bristled, but Dutch's steely gaze left no room for argument. She nodded in acquiescence.

"I'll speak with Gabe about watching the school," Dutch said.

Joel looked up at the deputies, comforted by their strong presence and reassurances. Dorinda managed a small, grateful smile.

"Mama, can we go to school now?" Joel asked quietly.

She squeezed his hand and managed a smile. "Of course. I think we've had enough excitement for now."

"I'll walk you there," Dutch said, opening the jail door.

They stepped outside and onto the bustling boardwalk. Dorinda scanned the street before heading in the direction of the school, gripping Joel's hand.

Dutch and Hawke stepped outside after Dorinda and Joel were safe inside the schoolhouse. As deputies, it was their sworn duty to protect the townspeople, and the mysterious woman's ominous appearance demanded more investigation.

"Where should we start looking?" Hawke scanned the busy main street.

Dutch rubbed his chin. "Let's ask around in the saloons. Maybe someone will recognize her description and know where she's from."

They took spots at one end of the bar in Finn's, glancing around at the people inside. "Where should we start?" Dutch asked.

Instead of answering, Hawke straightened away from the bar, walking into the center of the saloon.

"Pardon me," Hawke called out. Getting everyone's attention, he described the woman who'd accosted Dorinda and Joel. "Has anyone seen her, or know where she's staying?"

The men shook their heads or went back to what they were doing without responding.

Hawke sighed. Another dead end. They moved on to the Dixie, where he repeated what was said at Finn's. After a moment of silence, they got their first lead.

"I may know who she is." The man sat alone with a drink in front of him. "Strange looking woman. Saw her walking on the boardwalk about an hour ago. She was holding a sack."

"Did you see which way she went?" Hawke asked.

"Last I saw, she was walking past the school and out of town."

Dutch and Hawke thanked him and headed outside. "Let's get our horses and ride south," Dutch suggested. "We should stop by the jail and let Gabe know what we're doing."

Gabe wasn't in the jail, but Zeke Boudreaux was. "I'll let him know what you're doing when he gets in, Dutch."

"Thanks, Zeke."

Saddling their horses, they rode south of town, searching beyond the main trail.

After an hour of following tracks, Dutch grew impatient. That's when he spotted a woman walking alone on a footpath a good distance away from the trail. Hawke saw her, too.

"Let's make sure she's the one we're after," Dutch said.

Spurring their horses, they crossed the distance before she realized they were upon her. Reining to a stop, they slid to the ground. They rushed to either side of her.

"We need to speak with you," Hawke said. "Who are you, and what do you want with the schoolteacher and her boy?"

The woman gazed back and forth between the two

deputies, an unsettled glint in her eyes. The woman's raspy voice sent a chill down Dutch's spine when she spoke.

"I mean no harm to the teacher or the boy. I only wish to help."

Dutch scowled. "Help? By skulking around and frightening innocent folk? I find that hard to believe."

The woman sighed. "I know my presence is unsettling. But I come with information to protect them both from future misfortune."

Hawke stepped forward, his expression stern. "What is your name?"

"Violet."

"All right, Violet," Hawke said. "If you want to help, then talk straight."

The woman nodded, her gaze darting between them. "All right. I recognized the boy from before he went missing. I know who took him that day."

Dutch tensed, his eyes boring into the woman's. "You know who abducted the boy? Tell us."

"Patience," she croaked, raising a bony hand. "All will be revealed soon. Take me to the woman. It is to her I must tell this tale."

Hawke and Dutch exchanged uneasy glances. The woman was unsettling. Still, if she did have answers about Joel's disappearance, they had to pursue it.

"All right," Dutch said. "We'll take you to speak with Mrs. Heaton. But be warned, if you upset her, we'll end the conversation, and you'll have to answer our questions inside a cell at the jail."

Eyes flashing, she gave a slow nod. "I understand."

Dutch and Hawke escorted the mysterious woman to the schoolhouse, where Dorinda was finishing for the day. She froze when they entered, her eyes wide.

"You found her." She placed a hand on Joel's shoulder. He hovered close, clutching her skirt.

Dutch took Dorinda's arm. "She claims to have information about Joel's disappearance. Says she knows who took him."

Swaying, her face paled. For weeks, she'd agonized over the unknown details surrounding her son's disappearance. She glanced at the unnerving woman, wondering if she could trust what she said. As if reading her mind, Dutch lowered his voice.

"It's worth listening to what she has to say."

"All right, but I don't want Joel to listen."

Dutch turned toward Hawke. "Do you mind taking Joel outside?"

"Not at all."

"Mama, I want to stay with you."

She knelt down. "I understand, Joel, but I need you to go with Deputy DeBell. This won't take long, then we'll walk home."

"Come on, son." Hawke held out his hand. "We'll go to the boardinghouse and have some pie."

The corners of Joel's eyes crinkled. "All right." With a last look at his mother, he took Hawke's hand.

The woman stepped forward, removing her tattered black hood. Up close, her weathered face didn't seem so severe.

"Why don't both you ladies sit down?" When they

were settled, he took a position between them. "Dorinda, this is Violet." He motioned for the older woman to go ahead.

"What I have to say may be difficult to hear," Violet warned. "Many years ago, I served as a housekeeper for a troubled man named Jedidiah Grimes and his family."

Dorinda stiffened at the name. She'd heard of him. Jedidiah was a recluse who lived in a ramshackle cabin outside town. Rumors had long swirled about him.

Violet continued. "Jedidiah was not stable. He would rant to himself, becoming violent at times. I needed the work, so I stayed, but I kept my distance from him." She took a shuddering breath. "His family died in a buggy accident while I worked for him. He became worse afterward. He frightened me, so I quit."

She stared down at her hands. "Not long ago, when I walked past his cabin, I heard the voice of a child. I crept to the window and looked inside. Your son sat on the dirty floor, crying. I walked home, but couldn't stay away. Early one morning, I returned. The boy was in the same place, asleep on the floor. I couldn't see Jedidiah. I snuck inside and took your son with me."

Dorinda swiped at the moisture on her face. "Thank you."

"How did he act when you took him, Violet?" Dutch asked.

"He was scared and tried to get away. My grip was

too tight for him. When we reached my house, he refused to go inside. I gave him bread and butter, then took him to town. I left him close to the school."

Dorinda couldn't talk, her throat thick with emotion. The answers she'd sought were now before her.

Violet lifted a gnarled hand, then lowered it to her lap. "I am sorry. I should have come forward sooner." She bowed her head.

Dorinda's voice vibrated with emotion. "You rescued my son, putting yourself at risk. I'm grateful you're here now."

Her mind reeled as she processed what she'd heard. All this time, she'd blamed herself for his disappearance. In some ways, she'd always believed it was her fault. The guilt had nearly crushed her spirit. She looked at Dutch.

"What will happen to Mr. Grimes? Will he be arrested?"

Dutch placed a comforting hand on Dorinda's shoulder. "I'll talk to Gabe. Something will be done about him. I guarantee you he won't ever do this to another child."

Chapter Fourteen

"No one will get near either of you again," Dutch added with firm resolve. His imposing presence seemed to fill the room.

Dorinda nodded, her tension easing as she absorbed Dutch's reassuring words.

"I'm going to escort Violet outside and ask Hawke to take her back home."

"I'll go with you." Dorinda retrieved the bag she used to hold notes and supplies, leaving everything else for tomorrow.

Joel peered up as his mother, Violet, and Dutch left the schoolhouse and joined them. He eyed the older woman, uncertainty in his eyes. He moved close to Dorinda while Dutch took Hawke aside so they could talk. A moment later, Hawke left with Violet.

"Do you think she'll come back, Mama?" His voice was small but steady.

Dorinda cupped his cheek. "I don't know, sweetheart. Did she harm you?" She glanced over at Dutch.

Joel shook his head. "No."

"What about the old man, son? He's the one who took you, right?" Dutch asked, watching Joel's reaction.

Joel grew silent, clutching his mother's hand in a firm grip. "He made me sit on the floor. It was dirty."

"Did he feed you?" Dutch persisted.

"No. I just stayed on the floor." His shoulders trembled as he spoke. "I slept on the floor, too."

"The woman, Violet, said she took you away early in the morning. Do you remember that?"

Joel looked at Dutch and nodded. "Yes. She helped me get away from him. Do you think the man will come again, Dutch?"

"We won't let him get anywhere near you, son."

Joel seemed to take some comfort from Dutch's confidence. He leaned into Dorinda's side.

She ran her fingers through his hair. As she held him close, she felt the last threads of lingering guilt over his disappearance begin to loosen.

She met Dutch's eyes. "Thank you," she said softly. "For everything."

He smiled down at her. "You know you don't have to thank me, Dorinda. I would've helped you whether I was a deputy or not. How about I walk the two of you home?"

As they left the school grounds to cross Frontier Street, none of them saw the lone man standing across the street, his gaze following the trio.

Jared Heaton stood in the shadows of the covered boardwalk, watching his family walk home from school. His son, Joel, held his mother's hand while Dorinda and Dutch McFarlin talked. Jared's heart ached as he observed the happy trio, a family unit to which he no longer belonged.

How he wished he could turn back the clock to simpler times. He thought back to when it was the three of them living a quiet life on their farm. Dorinda would sing as she hung the laundry out to dry while Joel played stickball in the yard. Jared would come in from the fields at dusk, sweeping them both up in his arms. They would share a hearty supper and talk about their day before retiring to the porch to watch the sun set.

Jared cherished those memories of his family, his heart full to bursting with love for Dorinda and their boy. He never dreamed he would one day jeopardize it all. But the pressure from the elders had been immense, and he convinced himself taking a second wife was his duty.

Now, here he stood, on the outside looking in. The damage was done, the hurt too deep. Dorinda's laughter no longer welcomed him home.

Jared sighed, sadness and regret washing over him. It was time to let them go, to allow Dorinda the chance to heal and Joel to thrive under the care of a devoted mother. He turned and walked away, leaving his broken family behind. There was nothing left for him in Splendor anymore.

Jared made his way back to the small

boardinghouse near the church, each step heavy with grief. He'd lost everything that truly mattered by betraying Dorinda's trust and breaking his promise to make her his one and only wife.

As he reached the boardinghouse door, Jared paused, staring at the empty rocking chair on the porch. It reminded him of Dorinda's favorite place to sit in the evenings, gently rocking as she hummed lullabies for their sleeping boy. Jared swallowed hard against the lump in his throat, blinking back tears.

Stepping inside, he thought of Dorinda's beautiful smile, her tinkling laugh, the way her eyes lit up when she looked at him and Joel. The joy was gone now, replaced by hurt and bitterness he knew sliced right through her.

Jared had to accept he could never undo the damage. Dorinda would never welcome him home again. Their family was irrevocably broken, and it was all his fault.

Wiping a stray tear from his weathered cheek, Jared stepped inside his room, knowing what he must do. With a heavy heart, he picked up a pen.

His hand trembled as he began to write the letter he hoped would bring Dorinda some measure of peace.

My dearest Dorinda,

I know there are no words sufficient to express my sorrow for the pain I have caused you. When I broke my sacred promise and took Clara as a second wife, I acted rashly and without thought of the consequences. I see now the irreparable damage I have done, not just to our marriage, but to your spirit.

In my blind zeal, I failed to cherish the most precious gift God gave me. Your love. My actions can never be undone. I pray someday you may find it in your gentle heart to forgive me, though I do not deserve it.

I have made the difficult decision to leave Splendor. You and Joel deserve a fresh start, without the shadow of my mistake looming over you. Know that I will love you always, even from afar. Please tell our precious boy that his papa is proud of the fine young man he is becoming.

I regret many things, but none so great as losing you both. I hope and pray you will find joy again.

Yours always,
Jared

With tears streaming down his face, Jared folded the letter and tucked it into an envelope. He would ask Noah to deliver it when the time was right. Grabbing his saddlebags, Jared took one last look around the simple room. He strode out the door without glancing back, leaving Splendor and his shattered dreams behind.

Dorinda stood motionless as the weight of Jared's letter in her hand settled over her. Without reading it, she could guess what he'd written. "Is he still in town, Noah?"

"I'm afraid Jared rode out of town about an hour ago. I'd best get back to the livery."

"Thank you for delivering the letter, Noah," she said, closing the door behind him.

She closed her eyes as a soft cry escaped her lips. Jared was truly gone. The man she'd loved so completely, who'd been her partner and her heart's delight, had vanished like smoke on the wind. She felt a comforting hand on her shoulder.

"Do you want me to go after him, Dorinda?" Dutch asked.

"No. This would have happened eventually."

Joel burst through the front door, his young face flushed. "Mama! Did Papa leave town?" He didn't wait for her response. "We have to go after him."

Dorinda grasped his shoulders. "No, darling. Your father made the decision to leave." She blinked back fresh tears. "We must live with his decision, the same as we have since we left the farm."

Dutch stepped forward. "Your ma's right. Your pa has had time to decide what to do. You must honor the choice he's made."

"But..." Joel's lower lip quivered. Dorinda gathered him close, exchanging a grateful glance with

Dutch over the boy's head.

After supper, once Joel was tucked snugly into bed and Dutch had left, Dorinda retrieved the letter from the bedroom dresser. Sitting down at the kitchen table, her fingers trembled as she unfolded the single sheet of paper and read Jared's words by lamplight.

Each word was a lance through her heart. He spoke of his deep regret and abiding love for her, even as he accepted their bond was irreparably broken. As she reached the end, tears streamed down her cheeks. She would never again feel the comfort of his embrace or hear his deep, beloved voice. Crumpling the letter to her chest, she wept for all they'd lost.

She didn't know how much time had passed before pushing herself up from the chair. Since leaving the farm, she'd cried more than any woman should. After a time, she'd believed no more tears could be shed over her lost marriage and their shared dreams.

Gripping the crumpled letter in her hand, she accepted there may be more tears to come, perhaps for years. She'd hoped and prayed for a better resolution to their bond, wishing Jared would reappear to make everything right.

When he did, Dorinda had the horrifying realization no matter what he promised, her trust in him had been broken beyond repair. Forgiveness could be given, not so with shattered trust.

Trudging to bed, she slipped under the covers, knowing sleep would be difficult to find. Not just tonight, but for many more lonely days to come.

The next afternoon, Dutch arrived, holding an envelope. "I received a letter from Hiram Carlson, my parents' neighbor in Charleston. He says they are doing poorly."

His forehead creased with concern as he sat down, scanning the missive. "Over their protests, he summoned the doctor to check them. Doesn't seem too serious, but he ordered them to bed until their energy returned. Hiram tells me not to fret too much or rush home, though. He'll keep an eye on them for me."

Dorinda set down a cup of coffee in front of him. "I'm sorry to hear about their poor health. It sounds as if they're in good hands with Hiram keeping watch over them."

Dutch nodded, folding the letter with a pensive sigh. "I hope you're right." He reached out and gave her hand a grateful squeeze.

A knock on the door had Dorinda rushing to open it. "Good afternoon, Mr. Griggs."

"Morning, ma'am. Just received a telegram for Dutch McFarlin. Deputy Hawke at the jail said I might find him here."

"I'm here, Bernie." Taking it from the clerk's hand, Dutch pulled a coin from his pocket, handing it to Bernie. "I appreciate you going to the trouble of finding me."

"No problem, Deputy. Well, I'd better get moving."

Scanning the message, his brow furrowed.

"It's from my parents' banker in Charleston. He says there's plenty of money in their account for any repairs or help they need. He's going to go check on them himself today and send word of what more can be done."

Dutch set down the telegram, rubbing his jaw. Dorinda studied his conflicted face, seeing the struggle behind his eyes.

"Sounds like good news."

"It is. Still, I wonder if I should head back east to make certain." His voice trailed off as he gazed around the comfortable home.

She reached out and squeezed his arm, before he surprised Dorinda by tugging her into an embrace. He held her for a long moment, neither wanting to let go. Finally, he stepped back, running a hand over his face.

"I should wire the banker back and let him know I received his message and will await further word."

Dorinda busied herself tidying up the kitchen, ignoring the hollow feeling in her chest. She cared for Dutch and probably loved him. The thought of him leaving tore at her heart. What if he didn't return? Still, she knew his duty was to his family.

Dutch watched her for a few minutes, wishing there was an easy solution. If his parents' health was declining, they needed him with them. He couldn't, in good conscience, remain here while they struggled alone.

"I'll send messages to the banker and Hiram, then wait for word."

She paused, meeting his eyes across the room. In them, she saw the same ache and uncertainty she felt inside.

Dutch walked to the telegraph office, his mind swirling with indecision. He needed more information before making a decision.

The door jangled as he entered the small office. The telegraph operator glanced up in surprise from his paperwork.

"Afternoon, Deputy. Do you want to send a reply to the banker?"

Dutch dug the crumpled telegram out of his pocket and smoothed it flat on the counter.

"I sure do. And another to my parents' neighbor."

Bernie nodded and pulled out a blank telegraph form. "Go ahead."

After handing over payment for the wires, Dutch headed outside into the late afternoon sun, feeling a bit lighter. He'd done all he could for the moment.

Chapter Fifteen

The morning sun glistened off the windows of the shops as Dutch made his way along the streets of Splendor. He tipped his hat to Stan Petermann, sweeping the boardwalk outside the general store.

"How are you doing, Stan?"

"Well enough. At least I'm not dealing with any more cattle tearing up the town."

Chuckling, Dutch continued on, glancing in shop windows and touching his brim to couples out for their morning stroll. Though he presented an easy smile, his thoughts were troubled. His mind turned to his parents and his obligations to them.

The thought of returning there caused a swell of conflicted emotions. His family home held so many happy memories from his childhood, playing in the gardens with his older brother, Lowell. It also held the bitter pain of loss and learning of Lowell's death on the battlefield. The ache inside Dutch had never fully healed.

He pictured his mother's rose garden in full

bloom, the heady fragrance filling the air. His heart ached to walk those paths again. He reminded himself the Charleston he remembered was a world away from the life he'd built in Splendor. He had a job he enjoyed and people he cared about. He had purpose here. If he returned to Charleston, would he ever come back?

A gnawing guilt filled his gut. He felt bound by duty to his heritage and family name.

He also felt bound to this scrappy town he now called home. Gazing down the street at the people beginning their day, he knew none were aware of the conflict raging inside him. With a heavy sigh, he adjusted his hat and continued along the boardwalk.

Dutch stepped into the sheriff's office, his mind still churning with indecision. He poured a cup of coffee and walked to the window, trying to distract himself.

A flash of blue calico caught his eye through the window. Dorinda. His heart lurched at the sight of her. She waved at another woman, unaware of him watching her.

With a pang, Dutch realized he would have to stop spending time with Dorinda and Joel. If he returned to Charleston, it wouldn't be fair to pursue a relationship. Not until he was positive about returning.

As she approached the jail's door, Dutch steeled himself, schooling his features into a mask of indifference. When she stepped inside, he avoided meeting her gaze.

"Good morning, Dutch. I hoped you'd be here. Are

you available to have supper with Joel and me this evening? It'll be simple..." Her voice trailed off as Dutch walked past her to the desk. He pulled out a stack of wanted posters and rifled through them.

"Dutch?"

Lifting his head, he didn't offer his usual smile. "Sorry, but I have other plans, Dorinda."

"Oh. Well, another time perhaps," she said. Puzzled by his aloofness, she lingered a moment, realizing Dutch had no intention of saying more. With a confused backward glance, she left the office.

Once the door closed behind her, Dutch released a heavy breath. It pained him to turn down her generous offer, but it was for the best. He couldn't risk letting her get close, not when he didn't know if he would stay or go.

With a bitter taste in his mouth, Dutch forced himself to focus on work. In his heart, all he felt was the sharp sting of regret.

Dutch buried himself in paperwork.

Several days later, as he patrolled the town, he spotted her leaving the general store. His pulse quickened as he stepped into the shadows, watching as she made her way down the boardwalk. He tried to ignore the ache in his chest, but Dorinda's crestfallen face haunted him.

"Dorinda," a voice called out. Dutch turned to see Nathaniel Burke hurrying to catch up with her.

"Hello, Nathaniel. How nice to see you."

Nathaniel's eyes twinkled as he fell into step beside her. "I was hoping I'd run into you today. There's going to be a social tomorrow evening at the church. I'd be honored if you'd allow me to escort you. Joel is welcome to go with us."

Dorinda felt herself blush. "We'd love to go with you."

They chatted as they strolled together. Dorinda's welcome reaction of the other man's attention made Dutch's jaw tighten.

Over the next few weeks, Dorinda and Nathaniel became a familiar sight around town. Nathaniel brought her flowers and showered her with compliments, his intentions clear. Dorinda seemed to enjoy the attention, though now and then, Dutch caught a flicker of sadness in her eyes when she thought no one was looking.

Despite Dutch's efforts to keep his distance, he found himself watching them, envy mixing with regret. He had no claim over Dorinda, he knew, but it didn't make seeing her with another man any easier.

With a heavy sigh, Dutch turned away. He knew his decision to stop spending time with her and Joel was for the best. In his heart, he wondered if it was too late to set things right.

Joel kicked pebbles along the dirt road as he walked toward Frontier Street. He was supposed to meet his friends by the creek and was already late.

Walking behind Suzanne's boardinghouse, he

could see the creek several yards away, rippling a path toward Wildfire Creek. Dante and the other boys were already there, some wading in the shallows, others climbing the big oak tree arching over the water.

"Hey, Joel!" Dante called, waving. The other boys looked up and shouted their greetings, too.

Joel felt a grin spread over his face as he scrambled down the slope. His friends always made him feel welcome.

"We caught some crawdads earlier," Dante said as Joel reached them. He pointed to a bucket filled with the little creatures, their claws waving at being captured.

"You've caught a lot already," said Joel. The boys gathered around, dipping their hands in to feel the crawdads' prickly legs tickling their palms. Their laughter rang out over the churning water.

Joel was glad to have found his place among the rowdy, good-natured boys. With them, he could be himself. Together, they explored the wilderness around Splendor, sharing adventures and talking about their dreams. At his age, Joel didn't have many of either. Still, he could listen to the others for hours about their plans.

When the sun started its descent over the western mountains, they headed back into town, tired and dirty, but happier than they'd been all week. Though he missed his father, Joel decided this might be where he belonged.

Dorinda busied herself sweeping the floor at the schoolhouse, trying to ignore the ache in her heart. Joel had run off with his friends, as he'd been doing for an hour or two most days after school. It warmed her heart to see him making friends. The friends kept his mind off wondering why Dutch didn't come around anymore.

It had been weeks since he'd pulled away, avoiding her company and keeping their interactions brief and formal. She missed their easy friendship, their long talks, and shared laughter. His absence left a hole in her heart.

Dorinda enjoyed her time with Nathaniel. He was an easy companion, funny and kind, and he could talk about any topic. Even with all those characteristics, she found herself longing to see Dutch.

As she shelved books, her thoughts kept returning to Dutch like a compass needle seeking north. She replayed their last real conversation in her mind, searching for a clue to what had changed. Had she said something to offend him? Or was it simply he no longer cared for her company?

Not knowing why he no longer wanted her company was difficult. Dorinda was not one to sit idly by while her life unraveled around her. Yet she knew confronting Dutch would push him further away.

With a sigh, she turned her attention back to the task at hand. The books provided their own small measure of comfort, their leather spines and yellowed pages familiar. She took solace in the simple routine of returning each to its rightful place.

At least here, among the shelves, everything made sense. The books kept their secrets, but they held no mysteries about where they belonged. If only it was so easy with people, Dorinda mused, to look at their bindings and discern their proper spot.

She could avoid Dutch forever and continue pretending she didn't care why he'd withdrawn from her life. No number of books could fill the void his absence had carved out.

As Dorinda slid the last novel into place, she made the decision she'd avoided for weeks. She'd seek out Dutch and confront him. It was a risk, but to carry on like strangers under the same sky was the greatest risk of all. She could not lose his friendship without at least trying to regain it.

Taking a deep breath, Dorinda headed for the door, determined to find answers, no matter the cost.

Dorinda stepped outside, wondering where to begin. Their paths had diverged so much these last weeks, she didn't even know if he still worked during the day or at night. Something else she'd have to find out.

She'd start with the jailhouse, she decided. Even if he wasn't there now, someone would know where to find him.

Dorinda gathered her skirts and hurried down the boardwalk, weaving between folks completing errands. More than one tipped their hat or bid her good day. She smiled and rushed on, focused on her goal.

Dorinda slowed as she approached the jail's front door, more nervous than she realized. What if Dutch refused to see her? Or worse, met her with icy politeness.

She wavered, unsure whether to turn back or go forward. Blowing out a shaky breath, she told herself she'd come too far to quit now. Dorinda opened the door before her nerves took control.

Inside, the air was cool, and the light dim compared to the bustling street.

"Hello. Is anyone here?"

Heavy footsteps approached from the back. Dorinda took a step back as Dutch appeared, surprise flickering across his face. For a long moment, they stared at each other.

Dutch broke the silence first. "Dorinda. What are you doing here?"

She lifted her chin, meeting his shuttered gaze. "I came to find you. We need to talk."

Chapter Sixteen

Dutch's jaw tightened, but he nodded. "All right. Come on back. I'm cleaning one of the cells."

Dorinda followed him toward the cells, acutely aware of his imposing presence in the confined space. He picked up a broom and began sweeping, waiting for her to speak.

She clasped her hands to still their trembling. "I want to know why you've been avoiding me."

He didn't lift his head. "I haven't been—"

"Don't," she interrupted sharply. "Don't insult me by denying it. Ever since you received the telegram and letter, you haven't spoken two words to me. I thought we were friends." Her voice cracked on the last word.

Sighing, he straightened to pass a hand over his face. "We are friends. That's why things are complicated right now."

"What's so complicated about friendship?"

He gave a hollow laugh. "You know it's more than that."

Her breath caught. What was he saying?

"I care about you, Dorinda," he said, his voice low and soft. "Probably more than I should. I've got obligations back east I can't ignore. It wouldn't be fair to either of us if I let this go further, knowing I may have to leave."

She stared at him, stunned. "You never said anything about leaving Splendor for good."

"I haven't decided yet. It's a possibility I have to consider." His blue eyes showed the conflict he tried to hide. "I'm sorry if I hurt you. I thought it would be easier this way."

She tried to absorb his words. He cared for her but felt staying friends would be selfish. Though she understood his reasoning, it still stung.

"I wish you'd been honest with me from the start. At least then, I could've made my own choices."

Dutch winced. "You're right. I should've talked to you instead of pulling away. I was trying to protect you. It wasn't fair to you."

She managed a small smile. "Apology accepted."

Hope flickered in Dutch's eyes. "Still friends then?"

Her smile widened. "Always."

The office door banged open. "Dutch, we got trouble..."

Both turned at the sudden interruption. Shane Banderas stood in the doorway, his face flushed.

"Sorry to interrupt, but we got a situation unfolding down at the saloon."

Dutch was immediately all business. "What kind

of situation?"

"Four cowhands from the Double X just rode into town, already deep in their cups," Shane explained. "Started harassing the women at the Dixie, making lewd comments. When the bartender tried to get them to leave, one of them smashed a bottle on the man's head."

Dutch scowled, his jaw tight. "Let's go. Dorinda, stay here where it's safe." He followed Shane outside.

Across the street, raucous shouts and breaking glass emanated from the saloon. The two deputies joined up with three more, Hawke, Cash, and Beau, then hurried toward the chaos, hands on their six-shooters.

Inside, the saloon was in shambles. Overturned tables, broken chairs, and shattered glass littered the floor. The four cowhands were still there, laughing drunkenly amidst the damage. One had the bartender by the collar.

"Let him go," Dutch ordered, giving a sharp look at the drunken cowhand. "You and your partners get outside. Now."

The one holding the bartender sneered. "Who's gonna make us? You and your puppy dogs?"

Tension crackled in the air. Then, quick as a snake, Dutch drew his gun and fired. A bottle on the bar shattered.

"Next one won't miss," he warned. "Get moving."

With muttered curses, the cowhands began moving. Dutch and the other deputies kept their guns trained on the cowhands as they staggered toward the saloon doors. They didn't relax their stances until they were out on the street.

Shane hurried over to the bartender, who was slumped on the floor, holding his head. "Are you all right?"

The man winced. "I'll live. Those cowpokes sure know how to throw a punch."

Shane crouched to help him up. "Let's get you to the doc."

Outside, the deputies checked the pockets of each cowhand before hauling them to jail. Whatever money the miscreants had left would help pay for damages in the saloon. Dutch and Hawke returned inside.

They surveyed the wrecked saloon, shaking their heads. This was the third incident with rowdy cowhands in as many weeks. Something had to be done before someone got seriously hurt.

Dutch holstered his gun, his expression grim. "It's time Gabe meets with the ranchers about keeping their men in line."

Hawke nodded. "Seems trouble's been brewing for a while. Those cowhands are looking for an excuse to blow off steam."

"If this keeps up, Gabe will have to ban them from coming into town at all." Dutch sighed. "I know that'll rile them up something fierce."

"Better than someone getting killed," Hawke muttered.

Dorinda watched from the jail window. When Dutch walked out with the cowboys who caused the trouble, she headed outside.

Waiting until he walked back inside, she left the jail, careful to put a wide path between her and the four cowboys on her way to the Dixie. She gasped when she saw the damage. Dutch shook his head and smiled when he spotted her.

She worked in silence with the deputies for a few minutes, righting overturned tables and chairs. The saloon was a wreck. Broken glass and spilled beer were everywhere. She grabbed a broom from behind the bar and began sweeping the floor.

As Dorinda worked, she kept glancing over at Dutch. She could tell his mind was burdened with worry, his brow furrowed in thought.

"What is it?" she asked.

Dutch paused, looking around. "This kind of destruction can't continue. Danged if I know how to stop it."

She nodded, knowing he always sought to make peace, though it wasn't always easy.

"Talk to Gabe," she offered. "If you lay it out plain, I'm sure he'll listen."

Dutch gave a faint smile. "I appreciate the vote of confidence."

He took the broom from her hand and began sweeping.

Dorinda bit her lip. She knew he was right to be worried.

She opened her mouth to offer further encouragement, but Dutch spoke first.

"Best if you head home while the deputies handle this," he said, not meeting her eyes. "I'm sure Joel is wondering where you are."

Dorinda blinked, stung by the abrupt warning. Instead of throwing something back at him, she grabbed another broom.

An uneasy quiet settled between them. Her thoughts swirled as she tried to make sense of Dutch's sudden aloofness. She wished she could help ease his burden, the stubborn man seemed determined to handle this alone.

For now, she would respect his wishes, even though it pained her. She hoped in time he would again see her as a good friend, not someone to be kept at a distance.

Children of all ages burst through the doors, dispersing in all directions. Joel came sprinting out, his face flushed with excitement. He waved to Dutch as he raced to join a group of boys waiting for him under a nearby tree. He watched from the edge of the schoolyard, a smile touching his lips as Joel laughed with his friends.

A moment later, Dorinda emerged from the

schoolhouse, deep in conversation with Amelia. He straightened, an involuntary flutter in his stomach as her gaze met his. Surprise flashed in her eyes before her face softened into a smile. Telling Amelia she'd see her tomorrow, Dorinda bid her friend goodbye and walked to Dutch.

"Fancy seeing you here," she said, her tone warm yet guarded. "To what do I owe the pleasure?"

He tipped his hat back, his eyes crinkling at the corners. "I was passing by and thought I'd walk you home. If that's all right."

Dorinda studied him a moment, trying to discern his motives. Then she nodded. "That would be lovely."

They fell into step together, ambling toward her house. "Joel seems to be fitting in well," Dutch observed, glancing back at the boy still talking with his friends.

"Yes, he is. Cole's boy, Dante, has taken a liking to Joel." She mentioned one of Dutch's fellow deputies. "I'm so pleased Joel is finding his place here."

She went on to describe Joel's new friendships, the animation in her face easing the residual tension between them. He listened, interjecting an occasional comment or question. As they walked, he found himself enjoying her company, the nearness of her, as he did before the issues back east became known.

Dorinda slowed as they approached her house. She turned to Dutch, her expression soft yet searching. "Thank you for walking with me. It was kind of you to come by."

He rubbed the back of his neck, feeling shy. "My pleasure. Uh...I was wondering if you'd join me for lunch on Saturday. We could meet at the boardinghouse around noontime. Joel is welcome to come, too."

She considered him, a crease forming between her brows. Then she smiled. "I'd be pleased to meet you."

"Good, good." He exhaled in relief. They lingered a moment, neither quite ready to part ways.

She drew a breath. "Well, I suppose I should..." She gestured vaguely at her house.

Dutch tipped his hat. "Right. Saturday then."

Their eyes held an extra beat. Then Dorinda turned and walked up the steps to her front door, Dutch watching until she disappeared inside. He headed back toward town with a lightness in his step, feeling he'd been given a second chance.

Saturday arrived in a flurry of activity as Dutch prepared for his lunch with Dorinda. He selected a table by the window with a vase of wildflowers, wanting to make the atmosphere as pleasant as he could. At half past eleven, he stationed himself where he could watch for Dorinda's approach.

Right on time, she appeared down the street, wearing her blue calico dress and bonnet. Dutch straightened, pulse quickening. This was his opportunity to show Dorinda she could rely on him. With a deep breath, he stepped outside to greet her, determined to keep his promise.

Dutch smiled as Dorinda stopped next to him. "Good afternoon. I already have a table."

He led her inside the boardinghouse dining room. Her gaze landed on the beautiful flowers and table setting. "My, this is lovely."

"I'm glad you're pleased." He pulled her chair out.

She blushed as they took their seats. Soon, Suzanne hustled over with menus. "What can I get for you folks today?"

They placed their orders and settled in to enjoy the meal. The conversation flowed easily, from Joel's new friendships to the ongoings around town. Dorinda's initial shyness faded as she relaxed into Dutch's attentive company.

Midway through the main course, the rumble of an approaching coach caught their attention. Dutch glanced out the window, then did a double take. His eyes widened and his jaw went slack.

"Dutch? What is it?" Dorinda asked.

He was already on his feet. "I'm so sorry, there's someone...I have to..." He was out the door in a flash, leaving Dorinda staring after him in bewilderment.

Through the window, she watched Dutch rush across the street to a figure waiting on the boardwalk. A beautiful, fashionably dressed woman with dark hair pinned up under an elaborate hat stood ramrod straight, giving instructions to the stage driver.

Dorinda's brows knit together. Who was this stranger who had Dutch so flustered? She intended to find out.

Dutch approached the woman with a mix of anticipation and joy, wrapping his arms around her and spinning her in a circle with a whoop of delight.

"Mary! I can't believe you're here!" Dutch set her down, holding her by the shoulders to look at her.

She laughed, her eyes sparkling. "I had to come and see for myself if the rumors were true. Deputy Dutch McFarlin? My, how you've changed."

They chatted for a few minutes about her trip from Charleston. Dutch looked utterly enthralled, focused on Mary as she spoke.

Meanwhile, Dorinda watched the interaction unfold from her seat at the boardinghouse window. She was stunned by Dutch's effusive greeting and overt familiarity with this mystery woman.

Unsettled emotions swirled within her as she tried to make sense of it. Who was this woman? An old friend? Or something more? Dorinda wrung her napkin between her hands, eyebrows furrowed.

Dutch was still engrossed in conversation, grinning from ear to ear. He seemed a different man from the one who'd been dining with her moments before.

It became clear he'd forgotten all about her and their meals. Whoever the woman was, she'd captured his attention in a way Dorinda never had.

She sipped her coffee, unsure of what to do next. Her plate was still half full of delicious chicken stew, yet she hesitated. If the woman was this important to Dutch, perhaps it would be best to walk home, giving them time together.

"How about I wrap the stew up for you, Dorinda?"

"I would appreciate it, Suzanne. I'm sure Dutch will return in a bit to finish his meal."

"Whoever the woman is, he certainly is taken with

her."

Dorinda's stomach lurched on the thought she hadn't wanted to consider. Yes, it was past time she left and let him enjoy his visitor. When Dutch was ready to explain, he'd find her.

Carrying the small bundle Suzanne had wrapped for her, she stepped outside. Across the street, Dutch's back was turned to her, all his focus on the woman who'd stepped off the coach. A lump formed in her throat, noting his arm draped over the woman's shoulders.

Chapter Seventeen

Dorinda watched for another minute to see if Dutch remembered their lunch engagement and made a move to return to the restaurant. When he bent to retrieve two bags from the boardwalk, then strolled beside the woman toward the St. James, she had her answer.

An empty feeling engulfed her at the look of pure joy on his face. She'd never seen Dutch so excited, so captivated by anyone as much as the woman beside him.

Dorinda wondered about their story, how they'd met, where she'd traveled from, and why Dutch had never mentioned her.

Walking home, she stopped in the general store for a can of beans and two potatoes. Her next stop was the meat market, where she purchased a quarter pound of pork and half a loaf of bread. Mr. Caulfield placed all her items into a canvas bag, which she'd return tomorrow.

The last stop was the bookstore next door. Though

small, the shelves were packed with a good variety of history, science, and fiction books.

As a teacher, her funds were tight, yet her gaze kept returning to a dime novel about a frontiersman who'd helped settle the West. She chuckled at the title. From her experience, the West was still far from settled.

Paying for the book, she stashed it in her bag. With nowhere else to go, she walked home, considering what to do with the rest of the day.

With Joel spending time with Dante, Dorinda had hoped she and Dutch might take a ride back to the lagoon. It was such a beautiful spot, and she'd so enjoyed their time there with Joel.

For a few seconds, she considered renting a horse from Noah, and riding out herself. Grinning, she shook her head. She was more likely to put away her purchases, grab her new book, and walk back to the creek.

Years ago, she'd heard Noah had built a bench which he placed next to the water. A perfect place to relax and read or simply watch the creek follow a path to Wildfire Creek.

Dutch set down Mary's bags inside her room and, out of habit, glanced around to make sure nothing seemed out of place.

"I'm famished, Dutch. Why don't we take our

lunch downstairs? The restaurant looks quite nice."

Lunch. The word jogged his mind. "Dorinda," he whispered. Dutch's smile faded.

"What is it?"

"I've done something terrible." He moved toward the door.

"Terrible?"

He explained about lunch with Dorinda, and how he'd run out on her when he spotted Mary. "I have to go to the boardinghouse and apologize."

"Is she important to you?"

The smile returned. "I'm going to marry Dorinda. That is, if she'll have me."

"Then we need to find her. I want to meet the woman who's captured your heart."

Dorinda selected a hat with a wider brim for her trip to the creek. In the canvas sack Mr. Caulfield had given her, she'd packed her book and a slice of fruit bread. On her way home, she'd return the sack to the owner of the meat market.

It was a fine afternoon for a walk. The blue sky was an impressive deep hue, setting off the scattered white clouds.

Passing the livery, she waved to Noah as he groomed one of the horses. Bernie Griggs sat outside the telegraph office, his feet tapping to a beat no one else could hear. A smile appeared when he spotted her.

"Afternoon, ma'am." Bernie lifted his hat off his head, holding it in the air.

"Mr. Griggs."

Continuing to the school, she glanced at the open yard and the building, which needed a coat of paint. The bell needed to be cleaned, and the steps could use a few more nails.

Considering ways she and Amelia could obtain the funds, Dorinda turned toward the creek. The bench Noah made was in sight, and she felt a rush of excitement at the prospect of an hour or two of reading. Alone time was almost nonexistent. Between school and raising Joel alone, her days started early and ended late with little spare time.

She glanced at the sapphire blue stream meandering through the trees before taking a seat on the bench. The rippling water created a relaxing backdrop for the book she opened. *Seth Jones, Captives of the Frontier* was by the same author of another dime novel Dorinda had read.

Her surroundings faded as she became immersed in the story. Within a few minutes, she'd forgotten all about the disastrous lunch with Dutch, and the woman who'd been responsible for the absolute joy on his face.

"May I join you?" The familiar deep voice pulled her from an engrossing scene of a group of outlaws chasing the book's hero.

Looking up, a slow grin appeared. "Hello, Nathaniel. Please do sit down. I'd welcome the company." It wasn't precisely true, but she did enjoy the time spent with him.

"What are you reading?"

She showed him the cover. "Have you read this?"

"As a matter of fact, I have. It's quite good." Crossing his arms, Nathaniel stretched out his long legs as he watched the water. "This is a nice spot."

"My favorite, even though I seldom have time to enjoy it."

"Where's Joel?"

"With a friend from school. He'll be home in time for supper."

"Excellent. I'd be pleased if you and Joel would join me for supper."

A generous offer, yet she hesitated before reconsidering. "We'd love to join you. Joel loves the meatloaf at McCall's."

"Understandable. Betts makes excellent meatloaf."

"It's her husband's recipe. And trust me, neither of them share how it's made."

He lifted a brow. "Truly?"

"Positive. He makes most of the food and desserts. She told me he hates talking with the customers, and she hates cooking. The arrangement works well for both of them."

"Well, I'll be." He returned his gaze to the water. "Has Joel ever fished the creek?"

"I don't believe so. Why?"

"I can see trout from here. If I had a pole, it would be in the water already. I'll talk to Joel about going fishing at supper."

Both turned at the sound of footfalls on the ground littered with dried leaves. She let out a breath at the sight of Dutch and his female friend. Both stood, Nathaniel holding out his hand.

"Deputy."

Dutch gripped his hand. "Burke." He looked past Nathaniel to Dorinda. "I've been looking for you."

She didn't respond, her gaze moving to the woman.

"I apologize for leaving you stranded at the restaurant."

"I was hardly stranded."

"Well, it wasn't right of me. I'd like you to meet my dear friend, Mrs. Mary Stevens. We grew up together in Charleston. Mary, this is Mrs. Dorinda Heaton and Mr. Nathaniel Burke."

Mary looked between them, her pretty features creasing into a smile. "How do you do?"

Dorinda mustered a smile despite the unease she felt. "A pleasure to meet you."

Nathaniel touched the brim of his hat. "Ma'am."

"Mary arrived unexpectedly on the stage. We haven't seen each other in years," Dutch explained.

"Since before the war," Mary added. "I'm on my way to San Francisco to visit my aunt, but I heard Dutch was living here. I had to stop to see it for myself."

"See what?" Nathaniel asked.

"Dutch in a frontier town. Growing up, we all thought he'd end up in a large mansion the size of his parents' home."

"He still might," Dorinda said.

Mary nodded. "Yes, he told me a little about the house and his parents' health. It seems we may get Dutch back in Charleston after too many years away. However, I must say, Montana is beautiful."

"Is your husband with you?" Dorinda didn't know why she asked. A man didn't depart the stage with her.

"Mary's husband passed on two years ago," Dutch said. "She has a daughter close to Joel's age."

"Her name is Etta, after my late husband's sister. She's taking care of Etta while I'm gone." Mary looked toward the creek. "I'm certain she'd love it here. My girl is no Southern belle."

Dorinda nodded, processing this new information. She felt some of the tension leave her shoulders.

"Dutch was just telling me you're a schoolteacher here in Splendor. How wonderful," Mary said. "He seems quite taken with your boy."

At this, Dorinda noticed a hint of color rise on Dutch's cheeks.

"Yes, we're so thankful to call Splendor home now," Dorinda replied.

"And you, Mr. Burke. Where are you from?" Mary asked.

"Originally, New York. I now call Splendor my home."

"My goodness. So many people from the east. How interesting. I'd love to hear more about how both of you came to settle here," Mary said.

"Dorinda, Joel, and I are having supper together this evening. Why don't you and Dutch join us?"

"Thank you, Nathaniel," Dutch responded. "We'd be pleased to join you."

Nathaniel looked at Dorinda. "McCall's at six?"

Dorinda hesitated, then nodded. Perhaps getting to know this old friend of Dutch's would help resolve her conflicted feelings.

Chapter Eighteen

Dorinda walked between Joel and Nathaniel to McCall's. Entering, they found Dutch and Mary already inside at two tables Betts had pushed together.

Nathaniel removed his hat, setting it on a hook. "Good evening." He pulled out a chair for Dorinda, seating her next to Dutch, while he took a chair beside Mary.

"This is my son, Joel," Dorinda said. "Joel, this is Mrs. Stevens."

"Hello, Mrs. Stevens."

"It's nice to meet you, Joel. Tell me, what is your favorite item at McCall's?"

"Meatloaf."

The men chuckled at the quick response.

"Then I'm going to order meatloaf, too," Mary said, setting aside the handwritten menu.

When Betts took their orders and left the table, her husband had five orders of meatloaf to prepare.

While waiting for their meals, they talked about

various topics. "Tell me what brought you to Splendor, Dorinda," Mary said.

Without giving too many personal details, she recounted the winding journey she and Joel took to Splendor. She mentioned her older brother, Spencer, who worked at the Pelletier ranch, and being offered the teaching position.

"Splendor is a welcoming town. They took us in with open arms," Dorinda finished.

Betts arrived with their meals, ending the conversation. The way all of them dug in, a stranger would've thought none of the five had eaten in days.

"Joel, you are quite right. This is the best meatloaf I've ever eaten." Mary took a sip of coffee, looking at Nathaniel over the rim of her cup.

As she ate, Dorinda studied Mary out of the corner of her eye. The woman had an open face that glowed when she laughed at one of Dutch's jokes or comments. Their ease together spoke of a deep, long-standing bond. She wondered why Dutch hadn't married her.

Finishing her meal, she glanced at him from the corner of her eye, startled to find him watching her. She had no idea what to say, so she said nothing. When everyone had finished dessert, Dutch stood.

"Nathaniel, would you mind if I walked Joel and Dorinda home?"

"Not as long as I have the pleasure of walking Mrs. Stevens to her hotel." He looked at Mary, a question in his eyes.

"I would appreciate you accompanying me, Mr.

Burke. Joel, it was a pleasure meeting you."

His face flushed. "Thank you, Mrs. Stevens."

"I hope we're able to get together again before I leave town, Dorinda."

"That would be lovely, Mary. I'll be at the school each day, but might be able to take a little more time for lunch. At the boardinghouse, as it's close to the school."

"Perfect. Shall we say Tuesday?"

"I'll look forward to seeing you again," Dorinda said as they walked outside. She stood on the board-walk with Dutch and Joel, watching Nathaniel and Mary cross the street.

"Shall we?" Dutch offered his arm to her.

She slipped her arm through his, an odd sense of belonging moving through her. Dorinda found she welcomed the comfort of being close to him. As much as she liked Nathaniel, Dutch was the man she wanted in her life.

Joel ran ahead of them, jumping and skipping, his arms swinging in the air. "Hurry up, Mama...Dutch, you're walking too slow."

They looked at each other, chuckling at his antics. Neither spoke for several minutes. She realized he was taking the long route to her house.

"I'm sorry about today, Dorinda. Seeing Mary after all these years." He shook his head. "I was stunned when she stepped off the stage."

"How long has it been?"

"Years. Since before I joined the Confederate cause. I left, and several months later, I learned she'd married an older man we both knew in Charleston. Excellent family, wealthy. A strong supporter of what the South was trying to achieve. Until today, I didn't know she had a daughter, or that her husband died of consumption."

"She's a nice woman, and beautiful."

He glanced over at her. "I suppose she is. You're much more beautiful to me, Dorinda."

Staring ahead, she felt her throat constrict, making a response difficult. He tugged her closer to his side.

"Does Nathaniel mean a lot to you?"

The question didn't surprise her, partly because she'd been wondering the same. "He's a friend. You're the one who means a lot to me, Dutch."

He stopped, allowing Joel to get a little farther ahead of them. Turning so they faced each other, he cupped her face in his hands before placing a soft kiss on her lips. Pulling back, he stared into her eyes.

"You mean everything to me, Dorinda. I want time to prove it to you. Let me court you. Proper courting, so everyone knows what's happening between us. May I court you?"

A grin formed on her face as she set her hands on his shoulders. Going on tiptoes, she kissed him.

"Yes, you may court me. When can we start?"

Dorinda awoke the next morning feeling refreshed

and optimistic. Sunlight streamed in through the curtains of her bedroom windows, adding to her excitement about the day to come. She hummed softly to herself as she dressed, knowing she'd be seeing Dutch soon.

After their conversation the previous evening, Dorinda felt certain of Dutch's affection. His reunion with Mary had given her pause. She now understood their history was firmly grounded in friendship. Dorinda was the woman who held a place in Dutch's heart. The thought filled Dorinda with happiness.

She pinned up her hair and selected a light blue dress from her wardrobe. It was Sunday, and she wanted to look her best for church. She knew Dutch would be at the house soon, and she was eager to see him again.

Waking Joel, she stoked the kitchen stove as he dressed. Their breakfast consisted of scrambled eggs with bacon, and coffee for her. Soon, Dutch would be knocking on the door.

Dutch was still laughing the following morning when he recalled her words, and the look on her face when she said them. It hadn't taken him long to respond they could start tomorrow with him escorting her and Joel to Sunday service. He hadn't slept so well in quite a while.

Walking along her street, he hesitated at what he

thought to be a man rushing around the side of a house. Stopping a moment, he continued to watch, seeing nothing of concern.

Reaching her house, he knocked, taking a step back when the door opened. "Morning, Dorinda." He tipped his hat, a smile transforming his features.

"Good morning." She felt her face heat and hoped he didn't notice.

"Are you two ready?"

"We are."

She slipped her arm through his, feeling her heart beat faster. At the church, they slid into a pew beside Nathaniel and Mary, with Joel wedged between Dutch and Dorinda.

"Beautiful day," Mary whispered, smiling at Dorinda.

Soon, Reverend Paige entered, raising his hands in an invitation for the congregation to stand. When the opening hymn began, Dorinda listened to Dutch as his strong baritone joined in the song. She sang along, her voice light and airy. Her gaze remained fixed on the man who'd come to mean so much to her.

The song continued, lifting spirits. When it ended, Reverend Paige began leading them in another hymn.

The door of the church slammed open, and a man burst inside, interrupting the singing. As the voices faded, he shouted, yelling in unintelligible rants and creating panic among the congregation.

Dutch turned to see the man, his hand sliding to the butt of his six-shooter. Though the reverend didn't allow guns in church, an incident several years earlier ended with him granting Gabe and his deputies the ability to carry them.

His keen eyes studied the man, assessing the threat. The stranger was disheveled, crazed eyes darting around the room. He was clearly not in his right mind.

Gabe and several of his deputies were on their feet, approaching the man. "Easy now," Gabe said in a firm, calm tone. "We are no threat to you."

The man swung around, clutching a battered rifle, his finger curled around the trigger. The congregation gasped, women stifled screams, while mothers grabbed their children, tugging them close.

"The devil's here!" the man shrieked. "I've seen him!"

Dorinda's heart lurched. She pulled Joel against her, prepared to shield his body with her own if necessary. Her gaze flicked to Dutch. His hand had closed around his six-shooter, but he hadn't yet drawn it from his holster. Inching into the aisle, ready to rush the man, he waited for what the stranger did next.

Gabe took a slow step forward, his hands raised in a peaceful gesture. "No devil here, friend. Now, I'm going to have to ask you to hand over the rifle...nice and easy."

The man swung the rifle toward Gabe, his eyes wild. "Not until I kill him! The devil walks among you!" he screamed again.

A gasp rippled through the congregation. Dorinda

squeezed her eyes shut, her arms locked around Joel. A shot rang out.

"It's him," Joel whispered, his voice trembling. "The man who took me."

Dorinda stared at the stranger, realization dawning like a bolt of lightning. The wild eyes, the unkempt beard. She should've guessed the man's identity. Jedidiah Grimes.

The same man who'd kidnapped Joel from the schoolyard. Dorinda had spent hours sick with worry and fearing the worst. To find him here, now—it was as if fate had drawn them together in the most unlikely of places.

Another shot sounded, and Joel whimpered, burrowing deeper into the folds of her skirt. Dorinda gritted her teeth, fighting to remain calm for Joel's sake, though her insides were churning with fear.

"The devil is here!" the madman shrieked again. "I'll send him back to hell!"

There was a scuffle and a shout, and Dorinda opened her eyes to see Gabe and Dutch wrestling the rifle from the stranger's grasp. He released a bone-chilling scream, thrashing and kicking as several deputies forced him to the ground.

Grimes let out a wordless shout of fury, writhing against the deputies who pinned him down. He was outnumbered, his resistance futile. Within moments, they had subdued him, binding his hands and hauling him to his feet.

"He's lost his mind," Gabe said. "Get him out of here before he hurts someone."

The deputies nodded, dragging him from the church. The congregation breathed a collective sigh of relief as Morgan Wheeler, Tucker Nolan, and Jonas Taylor escorted the man from the church.

Gabe turned to the crowd, raising his hands again. "Folks, I apologize for the disturbance. Please remain calm so Reverend Paige may resume the service."

Dorinda exhaled, her heart still pounding. She stroked Joel's hair again, whispering soothing words to calm his trembling. After a bit, his grip on her skirt eased, though he made no move to leave her side.

She swallowed hard, blinking back tears of relief. They were safe. Grimes was gone. But the terror of those few moments would not soon fade from her memory.

The congregation stirred, slowly emerging from their hiding places. A mixture of emotions rippled through the crowd, unaware of another tragedy beginning to unfold.

Nathaniel grabbed Mary as she crumpled, catching her before she hit the floor. His heart slammed against his ribs at the sight of the spreading crimson stain on her blouse.

"Mary!" He eased her onto the pew, panic flooding his veins. A bullet had struck her in the chest, blood seeping between his fingers as he pressed down on the wound.

"Help!" he bellowed, shouting over the chaos surrounding them. "We need a doctor!" He pressed down harder on the wound.

Dorinda was at his side in an instant. Her eyes

widened with horror as she took in Mary's pale face, the red stain spreading across her chest.

Dutch shouted orders to summon the doctor. Within moments, Drake Ralston hurried toward them, his medical bag in one hand. He took one look at Mary lying motionless in Nathaniel's arms and knelt beside them, all business.

"She was shot," Nathaniel said hoarsely. He didn't dare relinquish his grip on Mary, as if by holding onto her, he could somehow keep her spirit tethered to her body.

Drake nodded, gingerly moving Mary's blouse aside to get a better look at the wound. "Single rifle shot to the chest. Massive blood loss." He looked up at Nathaniel, his expression grave. "I won't lie to you. This is very serious."

"You have to save her."

"I'll do everything I can. First, we must stop the bleeding." Drake opened his medical bag and got to work.

Chapter Nineteen

Noah Brandt's wagon rambled down Frontier Street, the horses taking a straight line to the church. His hands clenched the leather straps as his jaw clenched. He would not be too late.

The wagon stopped in front of the church. Noah leapt from the bench, rushing to help Nathaniel and Dutch carry Mary Stevens out of the church. They came toward him, their faces etched in worry and determination.

He rushed forward to see a dark stain spread across the front of her dress, and for one heart-stopping moment, he feared the worst.

Then Mary drew a ragged, shallow breath. He knew they were running out of time.

Doctor Ralston burst through the church doors. "We have to get her to the clinic."

Nathaniel and Dutch set her in the back of the wagon. Nathaniel stayed in the back with Mary while Dutch jumped onto the wagon seat, waiting for Noah. Ralston crawled in beside her, pressing a hand to her wound, staunching the flow of blood. "Drive, Noah! Now!"

Noah scrambled onto the bench, snapping the reins and urging the horses into motion. The wagon lurched forward, bouncing and rattling over the uneven road. Mary whimpered, her eyes fluttering open for a brief moment.

"We're taking you to the clinic. You're going to be all right," Nathaniel said, hoping he was right.

The wagon sped around the corner toward the clinic, racing against time. The wagon bounced and rattled, jostling Mary's limp form. Ralston struggled to keep pressure on the wound.

Dutch gripped the side of the wagon, scanning the road ahead. His heart pounded in his chest. They couldn't lose her. Not like this.

The clinic came into view.

Noah urged the horses forward for one final burst of speed. The clinic drew closer until the wagon skidded to a stop outside the door.

The door slammed open as Doctor McCord rushed out, his brow furrowing at the sight. "What on earth—?"

"She's been shot," Dutch said, his voice grim. He and Nathaniel moved in unison, lifting Mary from the wagon floor.

McCord's eyes widened. He ushered them inside, toward a room with an examination table. "What happened?"

"I'll explain later," Nathaniel bit out. His face was pale, hands shaking.

McCord nodded, Ralston joining him. Both immediately set to work.

Dutch released a shaky breath, running a hand over his face. They'd made it in time.

Now, it was up to the doctors.

McCord worked swiftly, Ralston handing him instruments without needing to be asked. The bullet had pierced Mary's chest, dangerously close to her heart.

"The bleeding has slowed, but her pulse is weak," Ralston said. He frowned, brows drawing together.

McCord glanced up, gaze flickering to Nathaniel. The man looked on the verge of collapse, face pale and eyes wild. "You should wait outside. This will not be pleasant."

Nathaniel's jaw tightened. "I'm not leaving her."

"As you wish." McCord's tone brooked no argument. "But do not interfere."

Nathaniel gave a sharp nod. McCord returned his focus to the task at hand. There was no time to waste.

Nathaniel stood motionless as McCord and Ralston worked, their hands moving swiftly and precisely. His heart slammed against his ribs in a pounding rhythm. He swallowed hard against the bile rising in his throat, refusing to look away despite the blood and gore.

"Her pulse is stabilizing," Ralston said, a note of relief in his tone.

Nathaniel sagged against the wall, nearly overpowered by a wave of dizziness.

"Dutch," McCord called out. When he appeared

from the waiting room, the doctor motioned toward Nathaniel. "Get him out of here."

Dutch guided him to a chair. Nathaniel dropped his head into his hands, chest tightening until he could scarcely breathe. He looked up to find Dutch, his face etched with empathy and determination.

Nathaniel managed a faint smile, gratitude welling in his chest. "Thank you."

Dutch and Dorinda sat in silence while the doctors continued to work on Mary, offering support and comfort. Joel sat on the other side of his mother, wishing crazy, old Jedidiah Grimes had never been born.

The door creaked open, and Cole Santori stepped inside. "How about I take Joel with me and Dante. He can stay at our house as long as necessary."

"Thank you, Cole."

"No thanks needed. Come on, Joel. Time to go."

Joel sniffled, lower lip trembling. "Go where?"

"You'll be staying with us until your mama can come get you," Cole said.

Joel cast a look at his mother, who nodded. Hugging her, he dashed outside with Cole.

Nathaniel sat beside Mary's bed, clutching her limp hand in his. She looked pale and fragile, her chest barely rising with each shallow breath. His heart twisted at the sight. He didn't know why a woman he'd known for such a short time meant so much to him.

"The fever was so high, I thought she would burn up from the inside out," he said softly to Dutch, who leaned against the wall.

Dorinda had left for home after Mary came through surgery. The bullet had been removed, but she'd fallen into a coma.

He stroked a stray curl from Mary's forehead. "She was stronger than any of us knew. The doctors said her body needs time to heal." Nathaniel swallowed hard. "You have to get better, Mary. I can't lose you, too."

Dutch had heard all this before during the last twenty-four hours after surgery. All except the part about losing her, too. Not for the first time, Dutch wondered about Nathaniel's past.

"She's young and healthy," Doc Ralston said from the doorway. "Her body just needs time, but she has a good chance. Why don't you get some fresh air? It would do you good."

Nathaniel stood. "You're right."

"Mary's in good hands here," Ralston said. "You should get some rest, too. No use wearing yourself out."

He watched as Mary's chest rose and fell, the rhythm steady and strong, before leaving with Dutch. The two men stepped outside.

Nathaniel began to walk with no destination in mind. "I was married once before. Rosemary meant everything to me." He stared down at the ground, sighing. "She was diagnosed with consumption. The doctor suggested we leave for a drier climate. New Mexico or the Arizona territory. She refused to leave home."

They kept walking, Dutch saying nothing, waiting for whatever else Nathaniel wanted to share.

"I watched each day as she became lost in her illness, knowing one day she'd be taken from me. When she died, I decided never again to allow love into my life. I would never again feel such pain." Nathaniel came to an abrupt stop, facing Dutch, anger in his voice. "So why do I care what happens to Mary?"

Dutch shook his head. "Why do men come to care for any woman? I don't have an answer for you, Nathaniel."

He didn't look at Dutch as they continued their walk. Before too long, they came upon the livery. Nathaniel stopped, looking over the fence to the stalls. Turning toward Dutch, he held out a hand.

"Thank you for listening. I believe I'll take a ride."

Grasping his hand, Dutch didn't realize it would be a long time before he saw Nathaniel again.

Bernie Griggs dashed up the clinic steps, opening the door to step inside. In his hand, he clutched a telegram for Dutch. He glanced around, surprised to find the large room empty. Deciding to return to the telegraph office, he paused when the front door opened.

Dutch approached him.

"Got a telegram for you." Bernie held it up.

"Good news?" Taking it, he read the contents. "Seems bad news is all there is lately."

"You going back east?"

Dutch looked toward the door of the room where Mary rested. "I don't know, Bernie."

"You let me know if you want to send a reply. Hard place to be, Deputy."

"Yes, it is."

Bernie's gaze darted around the room. "I'd best get back to the office. You take care now."

Standing in the center of the waiting room, Dutch read the telegram from the banker again. His father's health was declining once again. His mother was stable for now. Improvements to the estate were being made. The banker ended by saying he'd continue to send updates.

Folding the telegram, he stuffed it into a pocket. He didn't know what to do. His parents might not be around much longer. Mary was in the other room fighting for her life. There'd been a time when she'd been as important as family.

He looked at the closed door. Beyond it, Mary slept in an attempt to recover from the bullet wound. If he left for Charleston, Nathaniel and Dorinda would look after her. If he didn't leave, who would watch over his parents?

The answer was simple. Nobody except a neighbor the same age as his parents, and a banker, who had no ties to the elder McFarlins except having their money in his bank.

The next time the front door opened, Dorinda walked in carrying a wrapped package. She held it out to him. "You need to eat, Dutch."

Nodding, he took the wrapped food, setting it on a chair beside him. Reaching into a pocket, he withdrew the telegram. "From the banker in Charleston. Read it."

She took the message, reading it, then looking up at Dutch.

"I have to go to them. But I can't leave Splendor now. Not with Mary..." He looked up at Dorinda, anguish etched into his weathered face. "What am I going to do?"

"Your parents," Dorinda said. She sat down beside Dutch, slipping her arm through his. "Mary has me and Nathaniel. Your folks only have you."

"But Mary might not make it," Dutch said, torn between the three people who needed him most.

"Mary's a strong woman. She has the best doctors caring for her. If you go, I'll send you updates on Mary's condition every day."

Dutch looked at Dorinda, gratitude and anguish warring in his eyes. "You'd do that for me? Keep me updated so I know how she's faring?"

"You know I will," Dorinda said.

The next morning dawned gray and gloomy, a steady rain falling from leaden skies.

Dutch came awake with a start, his heart pounding. For a moment, he couldn't remember where he was. Then he saw the chairs lining the wall opposite him. Sitting up, he rubbed his face with both hands and it all came flooding back. He surged to his feet, dread knotting his stomach.

Opening the door, he found Mary still lying on the bed, her chest slowly rising and falling with each breath. Drake Ralston was slumped in a chair, asleep.

Dutch touched Mary's cheek, relief washing over him at the warmth of her skin. Her color looked better, he thought, and her breathing seemed easier.

"Her fever's broken," Drake said, sitting up. "She's going to pull through."

Dutch closed his eyes, gratitude flooding his soul. When he opened them again, Mary's eyes were open, gazing into his.

"You're still here," she whispered.

"I'm not going anywhere until you can walk out of the clinic on your own."

The exam room door opened. "Is it all right if I join you?" Dorinda asked, looking between Dutch and Drake.

Dutch held out his hand, his fingers threading through hers. "Mary is going to be all right."

Dorinda smiled at her. "You're looking much better. Before long, you'll be ready to continue your journey to San Francisco."

Mary's gaze moved past Dorinda and Dutch toward the door. "Is Nathaniel here?"

Dutch glanced away, then back at her. "He had some work to do. I'm sure he'll come by as soon as he has time."

Her look told him she didn't know if it was the truth or a lie. "I know he has quite a bit going on. It was good of him to stay through the surgery, right?"

"So true, Mary," Dorinda said. "As soon as you're well enough to leave, Dutch and I will get you back to the St. James. I've already spoken to Michael, and he's moving your belongings to the first floor so you don't have to maneuver the stairs."

Closing her eyes, Mary gave a slow nod. "Thank you."

The whispered words told them it was time to let her rest.

Chapter Twenty

A few days passed before Mary was well enough to return to the hotel. Most of the time, she sat in a chair by the window, wondering why Nathaniel hadn't found time to visit her.

"You and Dorinda are going to spoil me," she teased Dutch, who was tucking a blanket around her legs.

"What else can I get you?"

"Nothing. Just sit down and tell me more about you and Dorinda." She motioned to the chair next to hers.

He sat, pulling his chair closer. "Not much to tell."

"You haven't told her how you feel?"

"I've had a few other things on my mind, Mary."

"None as important as letting her know you love her."

"I'm sure you're right. It's just, well...I want to be sure she feels the same."

Mary hesitated. "You're right, of course." She picked up a glass of sarsaparilla and took a sip. "Have you heard more about your parents?"

He glanced out the window, watching the wind rustle the leaves on the nearby cottonwood trees. "They're gone."

"I'm so sorry. When?"

"Father died the day you woke up from the coma, and Mother died the following day. Their doctor said it was the darndest thing since she wasn't as sick as him. I received the telegram a few days ago as I was packing to leave for Charleston."

They sat in silence for a minute, Mary considering what to say. "There was a time they were as close to me as my own parents."

He gave a brittle chuckle. "I know. They thought of you as the daughter they never had."

"I've heard of married couples dying within days or weeks of each. It's possible she didn't want to live without him." Reaching out, she covered his hand with hers. "They loved each other very much."

Dutch glanced away, trying to hide the moisture building in his eyes. "Yes, they did."

"Are you going back now?"

"Do you recall their neighbor, Hiram Carlson?"

"The old man who stood about seven feet tall? Had a beard to his chest?"

Chuckling, he nodded. "He sent me a telegram, as did the banker. The neighbor offered to take care of funeral and burial arrangements. Carlson spoke to them a few weeks ago. They told him what they wanted. Seems they never expected me to return." His voice broke on the last.

"They loved you, and were very proud of you, Dutch. Their wish was for you to find your own life and be happy. I believe you've done both."

Looking at the ground, he fought to control the wave of loss.

"What did the banker tell you?"

"What you'd expect. I'm their sole heir, though I doubt they have much left other than the house and savings. The banker is going to send an accounting."

"So, you're not going east?"

"Not right now. Hiram Carlson knows of someone willing to rent the house, but I'd rather sell the property. I'll never live there again."

"Are you certain? It's a beautiful place with so many wonderful memories." Mary took another sip of sarsaparilla.

"It was also the memories that kept me away all these years."

"Lowell," she whispered.

"Yes. Too many reminders of growing up together."

"Renting will give you time to make sure."

"No. My life is out here now. If I ever go back, it will be for a visit, not to stay."

She stared into her lap for a moment before meeting his gaze. "Have you seen Nathaniel around town?"

"He stayed right by your side during most of the surgery and while you were in a coma."

"What are you trying not to say, Dutch?"

He shook his head. "I don't know, exactly."

"If he no longer holds an interest in me, please say so. I've been through much worse than losing the friendship of a man I hardly know."

Dutch thought of what Nathaniel had shared. "He's a widower, Mary."

The look on her face told him she didn't know. "Oh..."

"She died a few years ago of consumption."

"The same as my husband. It's a horrible illness, especially near the end." Lifting the glass of sarsaparilla, she set it back down. "It must have been hard for him to see me in a coma. Even though we'd known each other such a short time..."

"He took his horse from the livery and rode off. No one has seen him since, not even the man drawing up plans for his property. Bull Mason came into town for a meeting with Nathaniel. Gabe told him to speak with me. We rode out to his land but found no sign of him." Dutch scratched the back of his neck. "Nathaniel doesn't seem to be the kind of man who'd run out on his responsibilities. Gabe has known him for a long time, and he said the same."

"I suppose it doesn't matter. As soon as the doctors say I'm ready to travel, I'll continue to San Francisco. Which reminds me. I must get a telegram off to my aunt and let her know I've been delayed. And another to my late husband's sister. She's taking care of Etta for me."

"Yes, I remember."

"Etta will want to hear something from me."

"I'll take care of the telegrams for you."

She leaned back in her chair, closing her eyes. "Thank you, Dutch. The information is on the dresser."

By the time he'd stood to retrieve the paper, Mary had fallen asleep.

Dutch, Joel, and Dante led their horses from the livery after school for the ride to Ghost Lagoon. Their saddlebags bulged with fishing poles and an afternoon's provisions.

Joel practically bounced in excitement at the upcoming ride. "This is going to be great."

Dante nodded, patting the neck of his paint mare. "We're going to haul in a huge catch today."

Dutch couldn't help but smile at the eagerness of the young boys. "Should be some good fishing up at Ghost Lagoon. We should get riding if we want to haul in all those fish you want to catch."

Dutch gave the girth straps a firm tug, ensuring they were good and tight. After packing the last of their gear, the boys swung up into their saddles, faces flushed with anticipation.

"Let's ride!" Joel hollered, laughing as his buckskin gelding surged forward. Dante kicked his mare, her silver mane dancing in the light breeze.

Dutch mounted his sturdy bay gelding, moving out to take a position up front as they set off along the trail. The afternoon air was warm, and sunlight filtered through the pines, warming their backs as they rode.

Joel glanced ahead at Dutch as they rode toward the lagoon. "Dutch, what will happen to Jedidiah Grimes? Will he stay in jail?" His voice shook enough for Dutch to know the boy still feared the man who'd kidnapped him from the schoolyard and shot Mary Stevens. It could take months or years for Joel to come to terms with what had happened.

Reining his horse to ride beside Joel, Dutch pondered the question before responding. "I surely hope so, son. The man is dangerous, no doubt about it. A few of the deputies are going to take him to Big Pine. The judge there will decide what will happen to him."

Joel nodded, chewing his bottom lip anxiously. "It's just...what if he escapes?"

Reaching over, Dutch gave the boy's shoulder a reassuring squeeze. "The deputies will make sure Grimes is delivered safely to Sheriff Parker Sterling in Big Pine, where he'll face the judge. They aren't going to let him escape."

Dutch sat tall in the saddle, his jaw set as he recalled the day in the church. "You'll be safe, Joel. I guarantee it."

Joel's eyes shone with admiration as he looked over at the deputy. If Dutch thought it would be okay, then it must be true.

Up ahead, the shimmering blue waters of Ghost Lagoon came into view. For now, he'd try to push his worries aside and enjoy the day of fishing with Dante and Dutch.

The sun shone off of Ghost Lagoon as Dutch and the boys reined in. Surrounded by rolling hills dotted with wildflowers, the secluded fishing spot was one of Dutch's favorite places near Splendor.

Dismounting, Dutch began unpacking the fishing gear. "Sure is peaceful here," he remarked, taking in the scenic view.

The boys grabbed their fishing poles. "C'mon, let's start fishin'!" Dante said eagerly, rushing to the water's edge.

Dutch laughed. "Hold on, you gotta bait your hooks first."

Dutch watched with a smile as the two boys plopped down in the grass and checked the lines on their poles. Their enthusiasm was contagious. He knelt beside them, worms in hand.

"All right, you two. Let me help you rig up," he said, spearing a fat nightcrawler onto Joel's hook. The boy beamed, impatient to cast his line.

Within minutes, they were ready. Dutch gave them a nod. "Go on."

Grinning, the boys jumped up and hurled their lines out into the placid water. They stared intently at the lines, poised for the first sign of a bite.

Dutch settled back against a tree, keeping one eye on the lagoon and the other on the boys. He lived for simple moments like these. With the town growing, taking a day to relax didn't come often. Their high spirits today were a welcome change from the somber mood permeating Splendor days earlier.

Dutch let the boys fish in silence for a few

minutes, content to watch their youthful enthusiasm. Soon, an idea came to him.

"You boys ever hear the story of how this lagoon got its name?" he asked.

Joel and Dante turned to look at him, curiosity piqued. They shook their heads.

"Well, listen up, and let me tell you," Dutch said with a grin.

The boys eagerly plopped down in front of him, rods forgotten for the moment. Dutch lowered his voice for dramatic effect.

"Legend has it, many years ago, a group of pioneers came through here on their way out west. One night, while they were camped alongside this lagoon, an eerie fog rolled in."

Dutch paused, scanning the misty water.

"Out of the fog, they saw shadowy figures gliding across the surface of the water. Ghosts of tribal warriors keeping watch over their ancestral land."

Joel and Dante's eyes were wide. They stared out at the lagoon as if expecting to see the phantoms appear.

Dutch stifled a chuckle. "Rumor has it two dogs disappeared overnight. Just up and...poof!"

The boys jumped, brows raised.

"The pioneers were so spooked, they hightailed it out of here first thing the next morning. Ever since, this place has been known as Ghost Lagoon."

He grinned at the boys' rapt expressions.

"So keep your eyes peeled today." He looked up. "The sky's beginning to darken. Who knows what those warrior spirits might be up to..." His deep voice trailed off.

Joel and Dante looked uneasily at each other. Soon, their competitive natures took over.

"I bet I'll spot the ghost first!" Dante challenged.

"Nuh uh, I will!" Joel shot back.

Laughing, they turned their attention back to their fishing lines, keeping one eye on the water for any sign of ghosts or fish.

Dutch smiled, leaning back against the tree once more. If a good ghost story kept the boys entertained, his work here was done.

Chapter Twenty-One

The late afternoon sun shone off the surface of Ghost Lagoon. Joel and Dante sat with their fishing poles gripped in tight hands, watching their lines with intense focus. Any moment now, they were sure to get a bite. Or spot one of those ghostlike figures Dutch talked about.

Joel's line twitched. He jerked up, reeling quickly. The excitement ended when an empty hook popped up. Some clever fish had stolen his bait.

"Dang it!" he cried in frustration.

Dante laughed. "Too slow, Joel. You gotta be quicker next time."

Joel scowled and rebaited his hook, casting his line back out into the lagoon.

"Oh yeah? I bet I'll catch the biggest fish today," Joel challenged.

"I don't think so," Dante shot back. "I'm the best fisherman here."

The boys glared at each other, determined to out-do one another.

As they waited for more bites, their conversation drifted to other topics.

"Hey, Dante," Joel said after a moment. "What do you want to be when you grow up?"

Dante looked thoughtful. "I don't know. Maybe a deputy, like my papa. Or a sheriff, so I can catch all the bad guys. What about you?"

"I want to be a famous explorer," Joel declared. "Discover new places no one's ever seen before."

"That would be something," Dante breathed.

The two friends grinned at each other, the endless possibilities of the future unfolding before them. For now, they seemed content to sit at Ghost Lagoon, waiting for fish and ghosts.

Dutch watched the boys as they bantered and dreamed together. Though they'd been through some dark times in their short lives, they still had the optimism of childhood. Seeing them happy and carefree filled Dutch's heart with joy.

The afternoon sun dipped lower in the sky, casting an amber glow over Ghost Lagoon. Joel and Dante peered at the shimmering water, still hoping to spot one of the ghostly figures from Dutch's tale. The lagoon remained calm and quiet, with no apparitions in sight.

Despite the lack of activity, the boys were reluctant to leave. They wanted to stay until the last possible moment. Soon, they'd have to pack up their poles and make the ride back to town before darkness descended on them.

"It's time we started back to town," Dutch called.

"Aw, just a little longer." Joel didn't take his eyes off the water. "We haven't seen a single ghost."

Dante chimed in, "What if they only come out when it's real dark? We can't leave yet."

Dutch chuckled. "What would your folks say if I brought you home late? We can always come back another day."

The boys sighed but began reeling in their lines. As they packed up the gear, Dutch kept a watchful eye on the deepening shadows around the lagoon. He wouldn't let anything happen to the boys, ghost or not.

With the last of the supplies loaded, they mounted their horses and set off down the trail. The surrounding woods were hushed and still. Joel and Dante took one last look at the lagoon, their thirst for adventure far from quenched.

Dutch led the boys down the winding trail, keeping a brisk pace as the sun sank below the distant mountains. He wanted to reach the edge of the woods before full dark.

Joel kept glancing over his shoulder as the lagoon disappeared behind the trees. "Do you think Ghost Lagoon is haunted, Dutch?"

"Could be," Dutch said. "Folks around here have been telling ghost stories about this place for years."

Dante's eyes went wide. "What kind of ghost stories?"

Dutch smiled, seeing he had their full attention now. "Well, besides the tale I told you earlier, some say a band of outlaws used to hide out near the lagoon long ago. One night, the sheriff caught up to them, and there was a terrible gunfight. The spirits of those outlaws are said to still roam these woods, unable to rest."

The boys listened, enraptured and uneasy. The surrounding forest seemed to close in as darkness descended.

A distant, inhuman howl raised the hairs on the back of their necks. Their horses whinnied and danced around.

"Steady, boys, it's just a coyote," Dutch said as his eyes scanned the gloom.

The eerie cries continued as they rode on. Though the lagoon was behind them, Joel and Dante kept glancing around, half expecting to see ghostly shapes dart between the trees.

Reaching the edge of the woods, they spotted the lights of town in the distance.

Dutch grinned, patting his holster. "No ghosts or outlaws are getting past me, boys."

They laughed, the tension broken. But the chilling howls echoed in their minds as they rode toward home.

Dutch sat at the desk in the jail, staring at the letter in his hands. His eyes scanned the words again and again, not quite able to believe the contents. According to the lawyer, his parents had left him a vast inheritance, including properties all over South Carolina, stocks, bonds, and their grand plantation estate outside Charleston.

Glad to be alone, he leaned back in his chair, running a hand through his hair. This changed everything. He'd always assumed his parents were comfortable, the same as almost everyone in the exclusive area of Charleston. This letter painted a far different picture. They'd been quite wealthy, with assets Dutch couldn't even begin to tally up in his head.

What was he to do with such an inheritance? He had no experience managing estates or investments, and the scale of it all left him reeling.

And what would Dorinda make of all this? He felt certain she loved him for who he was, not what he owned. Such staggering wealth could change the dynamic between them. Dutch pondered whether to tell her right away or wait. For now, he'd keep the contents of the letter to himself.

This inheritance presented almost as many questions as it did opportunities. Dutch refolded the letter, his mind swirling. He had much to consider. The lawyer had instructed him to speak of it to no one unless he had total confidence and trust in the person. For now, Dutch tucked the life-altering news inside his vest pocket, close to his hammering heart.

Rising, he stepped outside, glancing up and down the busy street. He needed some time alone to gather his thoughts.

As he walked along the boardwalk, tipping his hat

at several people, he spotted Gabe Evans exiting the telegraph office. An idea struck Dutch. If anyone could give advice about managing an inheritance and properties, it would be Gabe. After all, he was from a wealthy New York family and had experience overseeing his family's assets out east.

"Morning, Gabe," Dutch called, quickening his pace to catch up to the sheriff.

"Dutch."

"If you have a few minutes, I want to talk to you about something." Dutch lowered his voice. "A private matter."

Gabe raised his eyebrows but nodded for Dutch to continue walking with him.

"You know my parents passed not long ago."

"Yes."

"Their attorney sent an accounting with word I've inherited a sizable estate," Dutch confessed. "I'm still taking it all in. I don't have the first idea about overseeing properties. You have experience managing your family's assets in New York, so I was hoping you could give me some guidance."

Gabe let out a low whistle. "My best advice is not to go it alone. Have experienced professionals manage the day-to-day operations of the properties. But stay involved. Review reports, ask questions, and keep a close watch on the books. You'll need to find people you can trust to steward your inheritance faithfully."

The men continued to walk, Dutch absorbing the counsel Gabe provided.

"I appreciate you taking the time, Gabe. You've given me a great deal to think about."

As they parted outside the sheriff's office, Dutch felt the weight of the future pressing down. He continued walking until he entered the law offices of Francesca Boudreaux and Griffin MacKenzie.

Their clerk, Damon Broom, told him Mr. Mac-Kenzie was available and led him upstairs.

Griff stood up from behind his large oak desk.

"Dutch, good to see you. Please have a seat."

Settling into the leather chair across from Griff, he began laying out the nature of his inheritance, his discussion with Gabe, and his desire to manage the properties successfully.

Griff listened, asking several questions. Finishing explaining, he leaned back in his chair.

"Well, you've certainly come into a large estate, no doubt about it," Griff said. "There's much to consider in how to structure the ownership and oversight of so many assets."

He explained Dutch's options, his expertise proving invaluable already.

"We should also draw up a thorough will," Griff continued. "Have you thought about beneficiaries for your estate if anything happens to you?"

At this, Dutch paused. Dorinda's kind, beautiful face filled his mind.

"I have," Dutch replied. "I'd like to leave it all to Mrs. Dorinda Heaton."

"The schoolteacher." Griff smiled. "A fine choice."

As the meeting progressed, they discussed additional details. By the time they finished, Dutch felt a measure of confidence return.

He stood, shaking Griff's hand. "Thank you."

"My pleasure," Griff said, walking him downstairs. "Don't hesitate to come by if any other questions come up."

Dutch stepped outside the office, feeling a sense of calm wash over him. His next stop would be the telegraph office. He needed to get a message off to the banker.

Mary stretched from her position in the bed, wincing at the lingering soreness. Though her gunshot wound had healed well under the doctors' diligent care, her strength and stamina were still returning day by day.

She gazed out the window of her hotel room, watching the creek continue along a familiar path to the river. As they often did, her thoughts turned to Nathaniel. His handsome features and kind smile filled her mind. She missed him more than seemed possible after knowing him for such a short time.

Mary wondered if he'd found what he was searching for out on the trail. Or if he might return to Splendor someday. A sense of emptiness descended upon her, not knowing if their paths would ever cross again.

With a determined breath, Mary shifted to the edge of the bed. She put her feet on the floor, took another deep breath, and stood. The pain was manageable. She shuffled across the room, holding onto furniture and walls for support.

Though her body still healed, Mary felt her resilient spirit strengthening. She thought of her daughter, Etta, intensively missing the young girl. A part of her wished she'd brought Etta with her. Instead, she'd bowed to the concerns of her sister-in-law and others who insisted it wouldn't be a wise decision. Having lived through getting shot by a madman, she had to acknowledge they'd been right.

Mary set out to walk around the hotel room twice. Returning to bed after three rounds, she felt exhausted but satisfied with her progress. She was determined to complete her trip to San Francisco to visit her ailing aunt. They'd been close when her mother's sister lived in Charleston. Mary refused to let her die before they shared one more visit.

Chapter Twenty-Two

Mary awoke the next morning feeling refreshed and determined. Today, she hoped Doctor McCord would approve her to travel so she could continue her journey west.

After dressing, she ate breakfast in the Eagle's Nest restaurant, then began walking to the clinic. When Dutch spotted her, he rushed to stand in front of her, blocking her path.

"What are you doing?"

"Walking to the clinic. Doctor McCord is going to check the wound one more time. I plan to take the afternoon stage west." Mary tried to move around him, stopping when he continued to stand in her way.

"Why didn't you send someone to fetch me? I would've picked you up in a wagon. We'll go to the livery and borrow a wagon from Noah."

"Don't be ridiculous. I'm fine."

Releasing a deep breath, he stared up the alley toward the clinic. "Fine, but I'm walking with you." He offered his arm, which she accepted with a gracious smile.

"Thank you, Dutch."

Reaching the clinic, he continued to mull over her intention to leave on the day's afternoon stage. After visiting her aunt for a month, she'd come back through Splendor on her return trip to Charleston. Entering the clinic, Clay McCord greeted them.

"Good morning, Doctor," Mary said while Dutch offered him a nod. "Do you have time to check my wound?"

"Of course. Follow me." He opened the door to one of the rooms. Once she was settled, he examined the wound and area around it. "You're healing up nicely," he said.

"I plan to leave on the afternoon stage for San Francisco."

"You appear ready to travel. Be careful, and don't overdo it. And do not carry your own bags. Do you have any questions?"

"No questions. Thank you, Doctor." Mary smiled, thanking Clay once more before leaving with Dutch.

Once back at the St. James, he carried her packed bags downstairs. "Michael, does the hotel still have a buggy?"

"We do, Deputy. It's around back, beside the stable where we keep the horse. I'll have Jacob hitch him to the buggy and load Mrs. Stevens's bags. He'll take you to the stagecoach station."

"Appreciate it, Michael."

When Jacob stopped the buggy in front of the hotel, Dutch helped Mary into the back seat while the bags were loaded. Dutch took a place beside her for the short ride to the station.

"Jacob, have we met before," Dutch asked as they passed the general store.

The young man smiled over his shoulder. "Yes, sir. I lived at the orphanage before Mr. Brandt helped me get a job here. My friend, Marcus, works at the leather and tack shop Mr. Brandt owns."

"I'm glad to see you at the St. James. The owners are real good people."

Jacob nodded. "Yes, sir. Nick Barnett and Gabe Evans are great bosses. Sheriff Evans said he'd pay for my trip to New York if I wanted to work at one of his hotels. I just might do that."

After Jacob stopped the buggy and set the bags on the boardwalk, Dutch shook his hand, giving him a few coins.

"I'll be seeing you around town, Jacob."

"Yes, sir, Deputy. Have a safe trip, ma'am."

"Thank you, Jacob."

When the buggy turned around to return to the hotel, they saw Dorinda come running toward them.

"Oh, Mary, are you sure you're ready for such a long journey?"

"I'll be fine, Dorinda. My strength returns more each day, and Doctor McCord gave his approval. I do plan to come through Splendor on my way home."

"Plan to stay at least a few days."

"I absolutely will."

The stagecoach bounced and jostled over the rugged terrain, kicking up clouds of dust in its wake. Etta held on as best she could, more than ready to reach their destination. Mile after mile on the railroad and stage, her excitement rose as they traveled across the vast Montana landscape, the endless open space dotted with small homesteads.

She leaned her head against the window, watching the scenery roll by in a hypnotic blur. As her eyes started to grow heavy, the stagecoach began to slow. They must be nearing the next town, Etta thought. She sat up straighter, eager for a respite from the relentless rocking.

Spotting the town ahead, her excitement returned. The coach rolled past what appeared to be a school and livery to stop in front of the station. The driver hopped down and opened the door.

"Splendor, Montana, folks," he announced. "Thirty minutes to stretch your legs. There are restaurants close by." He held out his hand to those getting off.

Etta stepped down. Somewhere in this town, she might find her mother. Her heart pumped at the prospect.

Mary watched from several feet away with mild interest, wondering who her travel companions would be on the journey west. Then she noticed a young girl standing by the stage. The girl whirled around, her gaze locking with Mary's.

"Mother!" Etta cried.

Mary froze in shock. She was stunned into silence as Etta rushed forward and threw her arms around her. Over her daughter's shoulder, she saw a familiar face. Her late husband's sister, Alice, climbed down from the stagecoach with a sheepish grin.

"What are you two doing here?" Mary finally found her voice again.

Etta's eyes gleamed. "We came to find you, Mother."

Alice approached, giving Mary a gentle hug. "I decided Etta and I needed some adventure, too. I knew from your telegram you'd be staying for a while, so..." She shrugged.

"But...your social obligations," Mary stammered.

Alice waved a hand. "I've made arrangements. This is more important."

Mary felt a swell of conflicting emotions. She was overjoyed to see her daughter again. Still, their sudden appearance also disrupted all her plans. She'd been ready to continue to San Francisco alone. What now?

Etta clutched her arm, babbling happily about the long trip and how delighted she was to finally be reunited. Alice looked on with a relieved smile. Mary began to recover from the initial shock. She managed a genuine smile for her daughter.

"Well, it seems you've managed to surprise your old mother," she said. "We've got a lot to talk about." She glanced toward the station, seeing Dutch and Dorinda looking on with more than a little interest.

As the stagecoach driver called for the passengers to reload, Mary's mouth twisted into a wry grin. Her journey, it seemed, would have to wait. With Etta's arm linked in hers, she led them toward Dutch and Dorinda.

"Etta, Alice, let me introduce you to Mrs. Dorinda Heaton and Deputy Dutch McFarlin. Dutch and Dorinda, this is my sister-in-law, Alice Buckley, and my daughter, Etta."

Once greetings were exchanged, Dutch suggested the women have lunch at the Eagle's Nest while he returned Mary's luggage to the hotel. They agreed, all except Dorinda, who excused herself to cross the street to the school.

Dorinda's gaze drifted over the rows of bent heads, each child absorbed in their book. All except two. Joel and Dante sat with their chairs pushed close, heads together as they whispered and giggled. She crossed the room to where Amelia wrote on the large slate board. Touching her shoulder, Amelia turned around, looking to where Dorinda nodded.

"Again?" Amelia whispered with an exasperated sigh. "I've spoken to them twice. I'll separate them."

Dorinda pursed her lips. "I'll take care of it."

Enough was enough. She strode over to the boys, her footsteps sharp against the wooden floor. Around her, young heads lifted as she approached.

Joel and Dante froze, smiles fading as they sensed her presence. Dorinda placed a hand on each of their shoulders.

"Boys," she said firmly. "What's our rule about talking during reading time?"

Her stern tone made the other students glance up from their books, curious as to what would happen next. Joel and Dante squirmed under her gaze.

"No talking," Joel mumbled.

She nodded. "That's right. And what happens when you break that rule?"

Dante stared at his book. "We have to stay inside during recess."

"Mmhmm. Miss Amelia has already given you two reminders. Now, I expect you to show me you can follow our rules without me hovering over you." She looked around the classroom. "Celia."

"Yes, Miss Dorinda."

"Bring your book and trade places with Joel for the rest of reading time."

"Yes, ma'am."

"But, Mama, I mean, Miss Dorinda. We'll be quiet."

"Too late. Go ahead, Dante. You'll be sitting there the rest of the day." She looked at the other students. "I want complete silence from here on out. Understood?"

"Yes, ma'am," they chorused. Joel shot Dante a covert look across the room as if to say this wasn't over yet.

The students ducked their heads once more, the

room blanketed in silence save for the whisper of turning pages. Dorinda noted the lingering smiles and curious glances toward the separated boys. Their antics still lingered in the children's minds, a welcome distraction from their studious routine.

Dorinda watched the classroom as the students read their books. Her attention kept drifting back to Joel and Dante, who sat apart, yet seemed to communicate in silence across the room.

She saw Joel's lips moving as he mouthed something to his friend. Dante's eyes widened and he nodded before catching Dorinda's stern gaze upon him. He ducked his head, but his excitement was palpable.

She stifled a sigh. The lure of adventure called to these boys. She would have her work cut out for her, channeling their restless energy into more constructive pursuits.

Dorinda returned to the front of the classroom, casting her gaze over the now quiet room. But she sensed the undercurrent of curiosity sparked by the boys' talk of ghosts. This would require some careful handling, she mused. The seeds of excitement had been planted in fertile young minds.

By Dutch, she knew.

Dorinda kept a watchful eye on Joel and Dante as reading time continued. She could see they were still distracted, their books open but their eyes wandering around the room.

They seemed to have wordless communication, exchanging furtive glances and exaggerated expressions as if plotting something exciting.

Despite her reminders, their curiosity about the ghostly legends lived on. Dorinda sighed, admiring their robust imaginations. The allure of adventure called to them.

The students finished reading time, and the children put away their books. As they lined up to go outside for a break, Joel and Dante gravitated toward each other, whispering and grinning.

"Joel, Dante, let's chat a moment," she said, steering them to the side of the room.

She crouched down to their eye level. "I can see those ghost stories have sparked your interest. It's important to stay focused during reading time. I know it can be hard when you're excited about something."

Joel scuffed his boot on the floor. "We think it would be fun to camp at Ghost Lagoon and see if the ghosts are really there."

She nodded. "I understand."

Joel's eyes widened. "We could camp at the lagoon?"

"We'll see," said Dorinda with a smile, an image of Dutch lodged in her mind. He'd triggered all this with his colorful tales of ghosts, and he would be the one to satisfy their curiosity.

The boys grinned, visions of adventures dancing in their heads.

Chapter Twenty-Three

Dorinda stood at the sink of her rented house, wiping her flour-dusted hands on her apron. She watched Dutch through her kitchen window as he made his way up the street. She felt a flutter of anticipation in her chest at the sight of his familiar stride. Walking to the door, she opened it as he mounted the steps.

"Evening, Dorinda."

"Supper's about ready." She smiled, leading the way inside. "I hope roast beef, vegetables, and biscuits are all right with you."

"Suits me just fine." Dutch followed her to the kitchen.

Joel's face shone when he saw the deputy. "Dutch! Wait 'til you hear about my idea for the summer!" The boy launched into an explanation of his and Dante's plan to camp out at Ghost Lagoon to fish and watch for ghosts.

Dutch listened, absently scratching his beard. "Hmm, camping by the lagoon could be fun, but we'd have to plan it real careful-like. Make sure we had enough supplies and picked a good spot to set up camp."

Joel's face fell. "You mean we can't go right away?"

"Not just yet, partner. It'll take some time to get ready. If your mama and Cole don't object, we'll go one of these days."

Dorinda gave Joel's shoulder a reassuring squeeze. "I'm sure we can arrange something soon. Now go wash up. Supper's on the table."

As Joel scampered off, Dorinda met Dutch's eyes with a grateful smile. It was good to have a man in the house who cared about her son. She hoped Dutch would stick around long enough to make the camping trip a reality.

Joel couldn't contain his excitement as Dorinda tucked him into bed.

"Do you really think Dutch will take us camping at the lagoon?"

Dorinda smiled as she pulled the quilt up under his chin. "I don't see why not. Deputy McFarlin seems to have taken a liking to you."

"He's the best!" Joel declared. "We might see real ghosts over the water if we camp there. Me and Dante are gonna catch one in a jar to show everyone in town."

"Dante and I," she corrected. "Don't go getting

ahead of yourself," she cautioned. "You focus on having a nice safe camping trip first. The rest can come later."

"Yes, ma'am." Joel sighed, settling back against his pillow.

Dorinda leaned down to kiss his forehead. "Sweet dreams, my dear. Mind you stay in bed now."

"I will," he promised on a wide yawn.

Stepping from the room, she left the door ajar. She hoped Dutch would follow through on his word. The lawman had never lied to her or Joel before, making her think he just might take the boys camping.

She entered the kitchen to find Dutch had already tidied up the kitchen. Not seeing him in the living room, she stepped outside to find him enjoying the cool evening air.

He turned, tilting his hat back. "Joel all tucked in?"

She nodded. "He's excited about the trip to Ghost Lagoon."

"It won't be for a while."

"He knows it won't." She looked up at the deep cerulean sky dotted with millions of stars.

"Are you in the mood for a walk?"

She nodded, a hint of a smile touching her lips.

He stepped over to Dorinda. "Shall we?"

Slipping her arm through his, they walked down the steps and headed down the street.

"It sure is peaceful tonight," he remarked after a few moments of easy silence.

She nodded, inhaling the pine-scented air. "I can't imagine being anywhere else. My job is what I've always wanted, and the people are kind and helpful. It's the perfect place to raise a family." She paused, glancing over at him. "Is it the same for you, being a lawman?"

Dutch tilted his head in thought. "I suppose it is. The badge is a calling. Once you pin it on, it's hard to let it go. Still, some men tend to wonder if there's more out there for him."

"Have you?"

"Not so much. After the war, I worked for Allan Pinkerton before ending up here." He turned them down another street. "I've seen a good portion of the country and was ready to find a place to call home." He swallowed, thinking about his parents and the large home in Charleston.

"How did you know about Splendor?"

"You've met Luke Pelletier, right?"

"Yes."

"He was also with Pinkerton for a time. We worked on a case together. Luke talked about this place all the time. When I left the agency a few years later, this is where I landed."

He turned his gaze on Dorinda. "What about you? Have you ever dreamt of seeing more of the world, having adventures beyond this corner of Montana?"

She looked down, brushing a stray lock of hair from her face. "I'd be lying if I said I didn't. This is the farthest east I've ever been. Maybe when Joel is grown..." She lifted her eyes back to Dutch. "It's a dream, nothing more."

"Dreams can come true."

"Of course they can." She tilted her head upward, enjoying the evening sky. "Maybe my dream will come true. For now, I'm happy being here. What about you? Do you have any big dreams tucked away?"

He gave a wry chuckle. "Maybe."

"Are you going to share?"

"I am." Instead of telling her, he continued leading them along streets with houses on each side. Most of them were built by Noah Brandt.

They continued on in silence, returning to her place. Walking up the steps, he stopped her from going inside.

Dutch stepped closer, his expression earnest. "You're an excellent mother and wonderful teacher. The town is lucky to have you." He paused a moment. "You're also the strongest woman I know, Dorinda."

He reached out and gently grasped her arms. "There's something I need to say. I...I care deeply for you and Joel." His voice was hoarse with emotion. "You've brought light back into my life when I thought there'd be nothing but darkness. An empty, lonely life." He looked away for a moment before meeting her gaze. "I love you and Joel."

Dorinda's eyes widened, her heart pounding. "Dutch..."

He searched her face. "I want the light to keep shining. I want us to build a life together."

"I..."

"Marry me, Dorinda. Let me stand beside you as your husband."

She was speechless, stunned by the sudden proposal. "Oh, Dutch. I love you, too. And I know Joel does, too."

"Is that a yes?" His eyes glowed with hope.

"Yes," she whispered. "Yes!" She threw her arms around him, laughing.

Dorinda pulled back to look up at him, her eyes shining. "I can hardly believe this is real. Are you sure you know what you're getting into with me and Joel?" Her tone was light, but there was a hint of vulnerability in her voice.

Dutch cupped her face in his hands. "I've never been more sure of anything. The two of you are the family I never thought I'd have." His voice grew gruff with emotion. "I want to be there for you both, in the good times and the bad. I'll do right by you, Dorinda, I promise."

Leaning down, he kissed her, a deep kiss expressing all he wanted to say.

She placed her hand over his, blinking back tears. "And we'll do right by you. Joel already looks up to you so much." A teasing gleam entered her eyes. "When he finds out, he's going to be over the moon. I hope you're ready for an excited little boy."

He chuckled. "I believe I can handle it." Dutch

drew her close again, kissing her again, the promise sealed between them.

Dorinda woke early, a smile spreading across her face as the memories of the previous night washed over her. Dutch's proposal, his heartfelt words, the passion of his kisses—it already seemed like a beautiful dream.

Slipping from bed, Dorinda dressed in her plain blue frock. There was much to do before Dutch arrived later in the morning. She wanted everything perfect for when they told Joel their happy news.

The boy barreled into the kitchen just as she took a pan of biscuits from the stove. "Is Dutch coming today?"

She smiled over her shoulder. "He sure is, and he has something important to tell you."

"What?"

"It's a surprise, so no pestering me or him about it. You need to be patient."

As they ate, her thoughts drifted back to Dutch. She couldn't wait to see Joel's reaction when he learned Dutch would be his pa.

They'd cleaned up the kitchen as the sound of boots on the steps signaled Dutch's arrival.

She squeezed Joel's shoulder. "Ready to greet our visitor?" He was at the door in a flash, drawing it open.

Dutch grinned at the sight of Joel. "Good morning." He mussed the boy's hair, looking past him to Dorinda, exchanging a knowing look with her.

"Mama said you have a surprise for me. What is it?"

"Slow down. All in good time."

"Joel, let Dutch come inside. Have you had breakfast?"

He set his hat on a hook by the door. "I have. I'd take coffee if you have some already made."

She handed him a full cup and sat down at the table. He took a chair beside her. Joel edged closer.

"Sit down, son," Dutch said, indicating the chair next to him.

Dorinda gave him an encouraging look. "I believe you had some news to share?"

Dutch nodded, turning to Joel. "Your mama's right, I do..."

Joel shifted on the chair. "What is it?"

Reaching out, Dutch took Dorinda's hand. "I care a great deal about you and your mother. More than anything, I want to be a part of your lives."

Joel's eyes widened as he scooted to the edge of the chair.

"Last night, I asked her to marry me."

Jaw dropping, Joel looked between his mother and Dutch. "Marry?"

"Yes. We'd all live together in one house. What do you think?"

Joel's brows scrunched together, his mouth twisting in thought. "In this house?"

"A bigger one. You'd have your own bedroom," Dutch answered.

"What about Papa?"

Dorinda leaned toward him. "Jared will always be your papa. When we're married, you'll also have a Papa in Splendor. Papa Dutch."

A smile began to form on Joel's face. "So, we still get to go fishing and search for ghosts?"

Chuckling, Dutch nodded. "Yes."

"All right." He slid down from the chair. "There's no school today, Mama. Can I play with Dante?"

Epilogue

Two weeks later...

The energetic music of fiddles filled the community hall as the wedding reception for Dutch and Dorinda swirled with joy. Guests laughed and danced, toasting the beaming bride and groom as they made their way around the room, accepting congratulations and well wishes.

Near the back of the hall, Mary sat with Alice and Etta, half-listening to their conversation about the trip to San Francisco they had delayed to attend the wedding. Mary nodded along, but her thoughts kept drifting to Nathaniel's noticeable absence. She'd hoped he would be here to share in the celebration. Mary sighed, pushing down her disappointment. This was Dutch and Dorinda's day, and she would not dampen it with her melancholy.

Across the room, Luke Pelletier stood with his wife, Ginny, near the dance floor, clapping along to the fiddle music. He spotted his older brother, Dax, and sister-in-law, Rachel, making their way through the crowd toward them.

"Quite a celebration, eh?" Dax said as he approached, clasping Luke's shoulder.

Rachel smiled at Ginny. "Doesn't Dorinda look radiant?"

The two women glanced over at the beaming bride, her cheeks flushed as she laughed at something Dutch said.

"She does indeed," Ginny agreed.

Nearby, Bull Mason had his arm wrapped around his wife, Lydia's, waist, grinning as he tapped a booted foot to the music. "Silas Jenks sure can play the fiddle."

Lydia smiled at her husband's enthusiasm. "He sure can."

"If you don't mind, I'm going to talk to Luke," Bull said.

She nodded, used to the way he switched topics. "Go ahead. I want to talk with Dutch's friends who are traveling to San Francisco."

Across the hall, Tucker Nolan fidgeted as he approached his two closest friends, Morgan Wheeler and Jonas Taylor. The reception was in full swing.

"Hey, fellas."

"Tucker. Who do you have your eye on for a dance?" Morgan asked, taking a sip of punch.

"Haven't decided." Tucker winced at the lie. He'd been trying to get a dance with Rose Keenan, but someone always seemed to get there before him.

Jonas raised a brow. "Tuck, we know you're interested in Rose. Grab her for a dance."

Tucker hesitated. "Yeah, me and every other single man around here today want a dance with her."

"Stay close to her and bide your time. Amelia is sure Rose is attracted to you." Morgan finished the last of his punch. "I'm going to refill my glass and find my wife. See you boys later."

Jonas watched Rose twirl around the floor with a Pelletier ranch hand. "Rose is a fine woman. Morgan's right. Don't give up on a dance so easily."

Tucker nodded, buoyed by his friend's encouragement. Perhaps Morgan was right. Feeling emboldened, Tucker headed off to ask Rose for a dance.

As he made his way across the crowded reception hall, the hum of celebration was suddenly interrupted when the door slammed open. A tall, broad-shouldered man strode into the room, his spurs jangling with each step. He was dressed all in black, with a pair of polished six-shooters holstered at his hips.

He stopped, surveying the room with narrowed eyes. Gabe handed his drink to his wife, Lena, and walked over to the stranger with a furrowed brow.

"Can I help you? This is a private wedding reception," Gabe said in a firm tone.

The man turned his dark brown gaze on the sheriff. "I'm here to celebrate the marriage of an old friend."

Gabe frowned. "I'm going to ask you to state your business or move along. We want no trouble here today."

The gunslinger smiled, though the expression didn't reach his hard eyes. "Easy now, Sheriff. I'm not here to cause trouble. Just paying a social visit. Perhaps you could point me in the direction of the groom. Dutch McFarlin?"

Caught off guard, Gabe hesitated. How did this stranger know Dutch? Keeping a wary eye on the man, Gabe escorted him through the crowd. Many of the guests gave them a wide berth as they made their way to where Dutch stood with Luke Pelletier and Bull Mason.

"Sorry to interrupt, gentlemen, but this gentleman says he's looking for you, Dutch," Gabe said tersely. "Says you're old friends."

Dutch's brow furrowed as he looked at the man. A tense silence fell over the group as they waited for some kind of explanation.

He studied the weathered face of the man he hadn't encountered in years. Not since his days as a Pinkerton agent.

"Can't say we're friends," Dutch replied.

Luke shifted his stance, eyeing the newcomer with suspicion. He didn't like surprises, especially ones crashing his friend's wedding reception.

Seeing the tension rising, Bull stepped forward, using his imposing frame to confront the stranger. The two men stood eye-to-eye, staring each other down.

When violence seemed imminent, the gunslinger's face split into a grin. "Well, I'll be. Aren't you a sight?"

Before anyone could react, Bull had wrapped his arms around the man in a fierce hug. "Ford. I can't believe it," Bull exclaimed.

Turning to the others, Bull kept an arm around the man's shoulders. "Meet my brother, Ford Mason."

Dutch, Gabe, and Luke gave the man wary nods of greeting.

Ford ignored the guarded gestures. "Hope I didn't cause too much of a ruckus dropping in unannounced."

Dutch looked at Bull before shrugging. "You're welcome as long as you don't cause any trouble."

Bull placed a hand on Ford's shoulder. "I'll make sure he doesn't, Dutch. Come on, let me introduce you to my wife, Lydia."

Across the room, Mary sipped her punch, trying her best to enjoy the reception without thinking about Nathaniel. Seeing couples twirling around the dance floor reminded her of what she was missing. Refusing to fall into a melancholy mood, she joined Lydia, who stood with Ginny a few feet away. They chatted amicably about the wedding, the upcoming summer, and their children.

As Mary scanned the room, her eyes fell on the dark-haired stranger with Bull as the two walked toward the group of women.

Bull smiled at them. "Ladies, this is my brother, Ford."

Lydia's eyes widened. "Your missing older brother?"

Ford replied. "Afraid so, ma'am."

Bull introduced him to Ginny and Mary.

Ford touched the brim of his hat. "It's a pleasure, ladies."

"So, what brings you to Splendor, Ford?" Lydia asked.

His mouth quirked in a half-smile. "What brings any man to a new town, ma'am? Opportunity. Adventure. Maybe a pretty girl or two to catch my eye." His gaze drifted to Mary.

Mary shifted uncomfortably under his stare. She'd hoped this wedding would distract her from wondering about Nathaniel, not put her in the path of a rough-looking newcomer.

"Excuse me, ladies." Ford walked around the group to stop next to Mary. She looked up into Ford's grinning face.

"Mind if I steal you for a dance?" He extended his hand.

Lydia and Ginny exchanged uncertain glances. An unsettled feeling gnawed at Mary, but she forced a polite smile.

"Of course," she acquiesced, allowing him to lead her to the dance floor.

As Ford led Mary in a waltz, Dutch, Luke, and Gabe exchanged uneasy looks. The party had taken an unexpected turn, and Ford Mason's arrival made Dutch wonder what trouble was brewing on the horizon for Splendor.

Enjoying the **Redemption Mountain** books? Here's another series you might want to read.

MacLarens of Boundary Mountain historical western romance series.

If you want to keep current on all my preorders, new releases, and other happenings, sign up for my newsletter: shirleendavies.com/contact.

A Note from Shirleen

Thank you for taking the time to read **Ghost Lagoon**!

If you enjoyed it, please consider telling your friends or posting a short review. Word of mouth is an author's best friend and much appreciated.

I care about quality, so if you find something in error, please contact me via email at shirleen@shirleendavies.com

Books by Shirleen Davies

Contemporary Western Romance Series

Macklins of Whiskey Bend

Thorn
Del
Boone
Kell
Zane

Cowboy's of Whistle Rock Ranch

The Cowboy's Road Home, Book One
The Cowboy's False Start, Book Two
The Cowboy's Second Chance Family, Book Three
The Cowboy's Final Ride, Book Four
The Cowboy's Surprise Reunion, Book Five
The Cowboy's Counterfeit Fiancée, Book Six
The Cowboy's Ultimate Challenge, Book Seven
The Cowboy's Simple Solution, Book Eight
The Cowboy's Broken Dream, Book Nine, Coming
Next in the Series!

MacLarens of Fire Mountain

Second Summer, Book One
Hard Landing, Book Two

One More Day, Book Three
All Your Nights, Book Four
Always Love You, Book Five
Hearts Don't Lie, Book Six
No Getting Over You, Book Seven
'Til the Sun Comes Up, Book Eight
Foolish Heart, Book Nine

Historical Western Romance Series

Redemption Mountain

Redemption's Edge, Book One
Wildfire Creek, Book Two
Sunrise Ridge, Book Three
Dixie Moon, Book Four
Survivor Pass, Book Five
Promise Trail, Book Six
Deep River, Book Seven
Courage Canyon, Book Eight
Forsaken Falls, Book Nine
Solitude Gorge, Book Ten
Rogue Rapids, Book Eleven
Angel Peak, Book Twelve
Restless Wind, Book Thirteen
Storm Summit, Book Fourteen
Mystery Mesa, Book Fifteen
Thunder Valley, Book Sixteen
A Very Splendor Christmas, Holiday Novella, Book
Seventeen

Paradise Point, Book Eighteen
Silent Sunset, Book Nineteen
Rocky Basin, Book Twenty
Captive Dawn, Book Twenty-One
Whisper Lake, Another Very Splendor Christmas,
Book Twenty-Two
Mustang Meadow, Book Twenty-Three
Solitary Glen, Book Twenty-Four
Ghost Lagoon, Book Twenty-Five
Renegade Woods, Book Twenty-Six, Coming Next in
the Series!

MacLarens of Fire Mountain

Tougher than the Rest, Book One
Faster than the Rest, Book Two
Harder than the Rest, Book Three
Stronger than the Rest, Book Four
Deadlier than the Rest, Book Five
Wilder than the Rest, Book Six

MacLarens of Boundary Mountain

Colin's Quest, Book One,
Brodie's Gamble, Book Two
Quinn's Honor, Book Three
Sam's Legacy, Book Four
Heather's Choice, Book Five
Nate's Destiny, Book Six
Blaine's Wager, Book Seven
Fletcher's Pride, Book Eight
Bay's Desire, Book Nine

Cam's Hope, Book Ten

__Romantic Suspense__

Eternal Brethren Military Romantic Suspense

Steadfast, Book One
Shattered, Book Two
Haunted, Book Three
Untamed, Book Four
Devoted, Book Five
Faithful, Book Six
Exposed, Book Seven
Undaunted, Book Eight
Resolute, Book Nine
Unspoken, Book Ten
Defiant, Book Eleven

Peregrine Bay Romantic Suspense

Reclaiming Love, Book One
Our Kind of Love, Book Two

Find all of my books at: shirleendavies.com

About Shirleen

Shirleen Davies writes romance—historical and contemporary western romance, and romantic suspense. She grew up in Southern California, attended Oregon State University, and has degrees from San Diego State University and the University of Maryland. During the day she provides consulting services to small and mid-sized businesses. But her real passion is writing emotionally charged stories of flawed people who find redemption through love and acceptance. She now lives with her husband in a beautiful town in northern Arizona.

I love to hear from my readers!
Send me an email: shirleen@shirleendavies.com
Visit my Website: www.shirleendavies.com
Sign up to be notified of New Releases:
www.shirleendavies.com/contact
Follow me on Amazon:
amazon.com/author/shirleendavies
Follow me on BookBub:
bookbub.com/authors/shirleen-davies

Other ways to connect with me:
Facebook Author Page:
facebook.com/shirleendaviesauthor
Pinterest: pinterest.com/shirleendavies
Instagram: instagram.com/shirleendavies_author
TikTok: shirleendavies_author
Twitter: www.twitter.com/shirleendavies

Copyright

Made in the USA
Middletown, DE
08 September 2024

60573753R00137